*A
Harlequin
Romance*

OTHER

Harlequin Romances

by JOYCE DINGWELL

CORPORATION BOSS

by

JOYCE DINGWELL

HARLEQUIN BOOKS   TORONTO
WINNIPEG

Original hard cover edition published in 1975
by Mills & Boon Limited

SBN 373-01952-1

Harlequin edition published February 1976

Printed in Canada

CHAPTER ONE

ALL day the narrow blue bitumen of the Northern Territory road had unwound for Constance in a dead straight line. It was not surprising, she thought, relaxed behind the wheel of the small car, that its nickname among its travellers was The Unbent Highway. But what Constance did find surprising after her last inland visit was the change now in the surrounding terrain. Down south in Sydney they all had read about the abnormal rains and what they had done to the 'Inside', but to gaze at flowers as far as the eye could reach instead of stone-strewn, stick-dry desert, on emerald grass instead of gibber, was almost unbelievable.

She wondered how it looked from the air, the way she . . . and Yolande and Guy . . . had travelled before. The sandy creeks, she knew, had turned into rivers, some of them forty miles wide. And there was an inland sea.

But not to think about such diverting things now, Constance prompted herself, all that could come later, rather to concentrate on getting to Corporation City before the sun went down. Corporation City! Such a ridiculous name! She hoped that when the project finally settled that the tag would die out, and C.C. become its aboriginal Ukurrie again, meaning Ours, though it was not theirs any more, not the natives'; they had sold it to Anthony Vine.

It had been an amicable deal, since the rightful

owners had been ready to move out, anyway – no sacred grounds to stop them, no tribal taboos, and more amicable since Anthony Vine had paid them so generously. Constance remembered Yolande's astonished face at the sum that had changed hands.

'Does anyone really have that much money, Consie?' she had gasped.

Anthony Vine had, but quite unconsciously, quite unobtrusively, quite – well, quite perfectly, Constance had thought at the time. She did not know what she thought now.

But she had admired the man then, she recalled, missing a crossing kangaroo by inches, instinctively she had liked that big generous man with the frank blue eyes in the leather-brown face, with the smile that reached those eyes. Now ... once again ... she did not know.

All she did know was that she must reach Corporation in an hour. One thing she must not do in this delicate mission was start off on a wrong foot. Constance put her right foot down on the accelerator and ate up a few more kilos.

It was growing darker much more rapidly than she had anticipated, and now cared about. At Quartz Hill, her last fuel stop, the petrol man had assured her that she should make it by six at the most, but evidently his pace was quicker than hers, or perhaps his car abler. Not that she had any complaints about Lorelei, the mini she had bought from Mattie. Lorelei had been reliable, if bumpy, right from Sydney, but it was now getting towards six, and there was a dark cloud to the west, and dark clouds in the Territory were something she was not yet practised in. Constance put her foot down again.

She tried to concentrate, but thinking of Lorelei made her think of Mattie and the girls. Three girls, four with herself. How well, how really well they had got on together. When people spoke of old gangs breaking up, they usually referred to the male species, but their own quartet had comprised a gang, too, a happy gang, but now it was all over. Phyllida and Mary had been preparing to go overseas to try their luck when Constance's Corporation call had come, and Mattie had been about to be married. 'I'm offering Lorelei for sale,' Mattie had said, looking at Constance, for she knew it would be useless looking at Phyllida and Mary, and Constance had said at once:

'Sold!'

'Seriously?'

'Very serious. I've decided, for obvious reasons, to drive, not fly, to Corporation City.'

They all knew the story by now, Yolande's pitiful story, and had nodded their understanding. They had been saddened, with Constance, by the news of Yolande's accident, in spite of the fact that they never had met her; they had asked Constance why she did not go up to her friend.

'That's the crunch, girls, I'm not Yolande's friend. We just worked together for a period. Yolande must have much closer acquaintances, and I'm sure she had a family, so how could I go, without being asked?'

'But you were there before.'

'In the line of duty only. Oh, I'd like to help Yolande if I could, but we barely knew each other.'

Then the letter had arrived. Three letters actually, but all in the one large encompassing envelope. One from Yolande. One from the Corporation doctor who had not been in attendance when Constance had been there. One from Anthony Vine.

Yolande had written: 'I want you here, Consie, you're the only one I feel I could bear just now.'

The doctor, a Doctor Hugh Mason, Constance had noted, had said: 'I think it would benefit Miss Lawford very much if you would join her, Miss Searle.'

Anthony Vine had written simply: 'Come.'

'Will you go?' the girls had asked.

'I think so,' Constance had said. 'Only—'

'Only?'

'Only I don't know what lies ahead, not like I did before. Then it was simply work waiting ... meeting the promoter of that work, but now, well, how can I tell? I mean, I liked Anthony Vine.' (I liked him instantly, I thought he liked me, Constance could have added.) 'Now it could be altogether different. But of one thing I'm sure: I must be independent. Independent as to getting there, independent as to coming away. For Yolande as well, who knows?'

'You mean this Vine person could have turned into a depriving stinker?'

'No, I'm sure he wouldn't, but I've decided, for obvious reasons, to drive, not fly, to Corporation City.'

Constance had smiled at Mattie to whom she had just said of Mattie's car:

'Sold!'

They had all sat silent a moment. They had shared each other's life patterns – four girls in one flat generally do share confidences as well as tea and toast, but Constance's had proved the quartet's most graphic story. They knew that Constance had worked as secretary and sometime model to Guy France, who was designing all those new, exciting (if so far less than lucrative) clothes. They knew that Yolande already had been working with Guy when Constance joined them, modelling his richer, more dramatic offerings, and that Constance had only been called in for 'aprony' things. That had been Constance's own description. 'Dresses to go to market in, house shifts, aprony things. Things Yolande wouldn't have been seen dead in.' But Constance had smiled quite fondly as she said it, and they had known what she meant.

They also had learned that when Anthony Vine had started Corporation City he had started first of all with a lavish hotel. No make-do pre-fabs for him, but the real thing, and a very beautiful thing, right from the start.

'I have a theory,' Constance remembered him saying one day during that working week-end when she had looked a little dubiously at the lush gardens, expansive shrubberies and expensive fountains in this literal middle of nowhere, 'that it's better to entice people to a beautiful place than to promise to make it beautiful if they come.'

'With the salaries I've been told the Corporation is paying I should say the men would come, anyway,' Constance had suggested.

'But clear out the moment they filled their pockets. No, Miss Searle, I want to *keep* them here, and the only way to keep a man in a place is to keep his woman

9

beside him. "Whither thou goest" may work for a while, but it takes a great deal of love to embrace a remote desert as well as your mate year after year. For that reason we have to make it attractive for women; as good, if possible better, than where they came from. The Corporation bungalows I plan will be little short of luxurious, and here at the community hotel there will be everything a modern couple can ask ... cool vestibules, swimming pools, libraries, music rooms, a dance floor, visiting artists. Fashion shows such as you're staging now.'

It had only been a small fashion show, just as the visiting orchestra had also been small, but the number of women Anthony Vine had initially flown up to look around and see for themselves, women carefully chosen for their influence on other women, had also been small in number. They had been a hundred per cent delighted, Anthony Vine had later reported in satisfaction, and when their homes were built they would come north with their husbands, advise their friends to do the same. It had been a complete success, the Corporation boss had assured the two girls. He had had to leave at once to fly down to Sydney for more recruits, but he had urged them to take their own time in returning ... even wait until he came back himself. There was so much still to see, so much more for him to show them. It must have been her imagination, Constance thought afterwards, that she had taken his words and his direct look ... it had seemed direct ... as words and a look for her.

'The hotel is yours,' he had bowed.

'Yes,' Constance remembered Yolande agreeing

very thoughtfully. 'Yes.'

Constance once more checked her watch, estimated that bank of cloud. The climatic offerings this year had confounded the experts. Actually it should be dry for months yet, but it seemed there was no longer any meteorological rhyme or reason.

That crimson streak in the sky now, for instance, should ensure fair weather, but all Constance recognized in it was the same colour as the carpet Anthony Vine had laid down for his first female guests.

'Red carpet!' Yolande, on their arrival, had been delighted.

'Showing you your importance,' the man had smiled back.

'Does a mere male walk on it, too?' Guy, behind the two girls, had asked whimsically. Guy was the designer, the inspiration, without him there was nothing.

Anthony Vine had nodded genially, and they had all passed into the beautiful hotel.

That week-end had gone in a flash, Constance re-called now. The future Corporation wives had been flown up, been shown Corporation City, been shown where the bungalows would be erected and what they would be like, had been entertained with music and the haute couture predictions of a young and rising Australian designer.

Then they had flown out again. After them had flown Anthony Vine. Then after the Corporation boss, Guy, declaring he could spare no more time, with Constance.

But Yolande had stayed on.

Yolande had simply announced to Constance: 'I'm

11

not leaving.'

'But, Yolande—'

'I know what I'm doing and I'm over twenty-one.'

'Yes, Yolande, but are you sure?'

'I'm sure of what I want, Consie, so you can at least be sure of that.'

Constance had paused for a long moment, she remembered, and fumbled for the right words. 'If you're thinking in the same strain as I'm thinking, Yolande, it – well, it takes more than one.'

'Then you're quite right, pet. It has taken more than one.' Yolande had flashed her lovely tilted smile, her irresistible smile, but she had offered no more.

She had not come down to the vestibule to see Guy and Constance off, a silent Guy for all the success of his small show. When the young designer had told Constance at the end of the flight that he was opting out, trying his luck in the States, Constance had felt she had understood. She had seen Guy look at Yolande many times, and she had interpreted that look.

She herself had still waited for something. Exactly what she could not have said. All she knew, all she was sure of, was that there *had* been a meeting somewhere between herself and Anthony Vine. A kind of exchange, a mutual look, an understanding. Then days had passed and at last she had accepted the fact that she must have only dreamed it all. What Yolande had insinuated must have been true, otherwise Anthony Vine would have written, otherwise Yolande would have come back by now.

She had taken a new job and a new flat. The invoice

typing was not as interesting as the design description and part modelling she had done for Guy France, but the company of the girls had made up for that. It had all become a brief and fast diminishing interlude ... except at odd small moments when a man's frank blue eyes in a leather brown face had come back to her, or a new red mat they had clubbed in for had reminded her of a red carpet. But that was all. It had to be all.

Then a brief letter had come from the Corporation doctor, who must have been established after Guy and Constance had left, telling of Yolande's unfortunate accident some time ago. The girl had fallen down the hotel stairs and sustained considerable injuries, or so it was thought at this stage. Anyway, she could not walk.

The shock had been very sharp and very real. Yolande was the last person in the world you could associate with physical injury, but as Constance had said futilely to the girls, how could she intrude?

Then the packet with the three letters in it had arrived, and Constance found she was to intrude after all – though only intrude, she insisted to herself, by invitation. But because it could still be intrusion in spite of Anthony Vine's: 'Come', she had brought Mattie's old car, so she would be independent. Anthony Vine had seemed everything compassionate, everything generous and intrinsic, but that could still be imagination on her part as it had been for something else, so how could she be sure? If Yolande was unhappy, a car, one's own car, would be invaluable. She could take Yolande out for a day, even take her right away from Corporation City if it came to that.

13

But immediately ... and Constance saw with dismay that the light patter of rain that had accompanied her all the way from Quartz Hill was thickening ... she must get *to*, not from, Corporation City.

She accelerated. She put her foot right down – and ran into a rut.

It was a short but very deep rut. Constance tried reversing, but the back wheel could not make it. She put everything into a forward effort but to no avail.

She sat bitterly disappointed. She had wanted to arrive at Corporation City quietly confident, confident she could help. Now it seemed she would need help herself.

Vexed, frustrated, she turned the key in the ignition, for in the unsuccessful grinding backwards and forwards the engine had cut off. There was no response.

Again Constance tried, using all the tricks she had been advised by Mattie guaranteed to coax a purr from a sulky Lorelei. Nothing happened.

... Nothing, unless, and Constance looked in horror at the rising water in the floor of Lorelei, you counted *this* as something. She watched the level keenly. Climbing up or going down? A freak run-off from some saturated creek or here to stop? She scratched a mark on the inside of the door. No, she found presently, the water level was definitely ascending. As she sat now the murky wet almost reached her knees. I'll have to get out, Constance knew, feeling sick at the thought of abandoning her car, and she looked behind her to see what she could rescue from the back seat.

'No time for that!' the voice shouted at her through

the closed window, shouted so loud there might not have been any window at all. 'For God's sake, girl,' the voice said next, 'get out!'

It was a man's voice. That was all Constance could register. Mechanically she opened the door, gasping at the immediate inrush of water that she saw now must envelop her to her waist.

'Come on,' called the voice.

'I can't.'

In reply, the owner of the voice said: 'Then hang on.' He leaned into the cabin of the small car and lifted her out.

He wasted no time. Still holding her, he began moving forward, and from his heavy breathing Constance knew it must be a hard job. She could hear the swish of water as he pushed through it, and though he held her high, at times water still broke over her face. She could not see him. The little vision she did have, held tightly upward as he held her, only gave her a picture of someone large and strong struggling through obscure murk. At times he went into a rut, as Lorelei had, and then Constance felt water closing all over her, but he never released her, and he never gave up, not even when an uprooted tree slid past them, evidently gashing his hand, for the grey murk showed a red patch of blood.

Then he was climbing, climbing slowly out of it, waist-deep at first, and then to his knees. When he was ankle-depth he put Constance down, and they both turned and looked at Lorelei, slewed to one side by now, then, even as they watched, turning over several times into a deep ditch.

'Oh, no!' Constance cried.

'I'm afraid so.' There was no intervening glass to change his voice now, and it came subconsciously to Constance that she had heard that rather slow, rather deliberate timbre before.

'Will it go further?' she asked.

'No. The freak run-off has run away. But, unhappily, so has your car.'

'Could it be towed?'

'No, I doubt if the car would stand it.'

'But I have to get to Corporation City!' she wailed.

'You're there now, Miss Searle.'

Miss Searle? For the first time Constance really looked up at her rescuer.

'Not C.C. itself,' the man was saying, 'but pretty close when you consider this tall state of long kilos. Only thirty of them left now, I'd say.'

But Constance was not listening. Also, for the moment, she was not thinking about Lorelei.

'Anthony Vine,' she said quietly.

'Yes, Miss Searle.'

He was smiling at her. It seemed it was something he could do on a flooded outback road quite as well as in a luxury hotel. His eyes were as blue as she remembered, his face as leather brown. She had liked him from the first moment she had seen him, and that was the first instinctive thing she thought of now, but a lot of water had flowed under the bridge since then . . . oh, lord, why had she thought of water? . . . and it was different this time.

Different because Yolande had stayed on at Corporation. Different because Yolande had flashed her lovely tilted smile and answered Constance's warning 'It takes more than one' with a triumphant:

'You're right. It has taken more than one.'

Different because Anthony Vine had never got in touch, never refuted what he must have known would be implied by Yolande's presence and his own apparent acceptance of it.

Different because after months of silence, after a crippling accident, after doing everything together as those two would be doing things together, Anthony Vine must be, had to be – Yolande's man.

CHAPTER TWO

ANTHONY VINE had taken off his jacket and now he was placing it around Constance's shoulders. She started to protest that she was not cold, for up in these latitudes the weather only ever differed from warm to hot, then stopped. Looking back on her moment of discovery just now, her discovery of Anthony Vine, she knew that involuntarily she had shivered. Shivered at the difference between them this time, for now there was Yolande standing between. That was ridiculous, she tried to tell herself, there had never been anything, not actually, so why was she suddenly cold like this?

'How are you here?' She managed to ask it quite unemotionally.

'It is my place,' he reminded her.

'But thirty kilometres . . . it was thirty that you said? . . . away from Corporation?'

'It's still Corporation, or Ukurrie as I believe, like me, you prefer to call it, even if it's not the centre. We are, you must remember from your air flips that weekend, a very extensive concern.'

'Yes,' Constance said. But after a while she asked again: 'Why, Mr. Vine?'

'For heaven's sake make it Anthony. Tony, if you prefer. But not Mister. Not up here, Constance.'

'Anthony,' she agreed. 'Why?'

'A hunch. An intuition. Or' . . . tentatively . . . 'could we be in tune?'

'Not to the degree of expecting me to arrive by road instead of air,' she told him coolly. She felt she had to be cool.

'Yet I'm still here,' he pointed out, 'and don't ask why again, since the reason must be obvious.'

'Obvious?' she queried.

'Well, to be direct about it, Constance, you didn't know just what to expect here, did you?' he said bluntly. 'Whereupon you played safe and independent by bringing your own transport.'

'I brought it for Yolande as well,' she came back, equally direct and blunt.

'To a hotel already boasting more cars than people,' he reproached.

'I'm sorry, Mr. – I mean Anthony. You're right, of course. I didn't know what to expect. I didn't know how you were taking things, how Yolande was taking them. I didn't know anything at all.'

'Nor bothered to find out.'

'That's unfair! I wanted to, but it was not my place. Contrary to what you might think, Yolande has never been my close friend, otherwise I would have come before now.'

There was a pause. It was quite a long one. Then:

'. . . it was not of Yolande I was speaking,' he said.

'I don't understand you.'

'And yet I thought you did.' He spoke very quietly. 'I was sure you did.' The blue eyes were looking steadily now into Constance's grey ones.

'There was nothing to make you feel like that,' she returned at once. Until she knew more about everything she felt she had to speak like this. But she turned her eyes away as she said it, sharply conscious that she was lying. Right from the moment she had smiled back at this man that first day she had been aware of a glow in her, of a warm certainty that if she had stood in the darkest room that glow would still be there. *Show* there.

But why was he speaking to her *personally* now? He hadn't done so before. He had looked at her, and she had thought she had understood that look, but he had not said any of the things that he had just said a moment ago. Was the difference this time the fact that Yolande no longer stood comparatively beside her? Lovely, unforgettable, irresistible Yolande? Was it because Yolande could not now stand beside anyone since she was imprisoned instead in a chair? Was he a man like that? If the best no longer attracted, then turning to the second best?

Constance shivered again and Anthony Vine said: 'Look, it's no use watching your car break up, we'll get going.'

'Where?' she asked a little stupidly.

'To Corporation, of course, where else?'

'I really meant how?'

'I didn't fly here, which you should have done, and certainly would have done had I known what you schemed. No, I've brought out my waggon. Somehow I sensed you would be doing this, coming on your own accord in your own ... now ex ... car. But mine is entirely reliable. It's a four-wheel drive and guaranteed to get you any place. Come on before you start a chill.'

'Up here?' she queried.

'It does happen.'

The waggon was parked further along the wet bitumen. He opened up and she got in.

'What about my clothes?' she asked.

'Gone with the car,' he told her. 'You'll have to send down to Sydney, we haven't got round to a boutique as yet. But I'm sure Yolande will help you. After all, she has little need of them herself.'

She heard him distinctly but could not bring herself to turn and look incredulously at him, though incredulous she felt. She did not want to see those frank blue eyes she had once liked instantly emphasizing to her what he had just cruelly spoken, for direct, unadorned words like that had to be cruel. 'After all,' he had said, 'Yolande has little need of them herself.'

This man . . . this man could *not* be the man she had known before.

'How is Corporation City?' she asked, hoping he did not hear the choke in her voice.

'Bungalows up but wives not yet arrived. Thank heaven at least for that. I wanted a gay beginning, a promising start, not a—' His voice trailed off.

Constance sat stiff and unbelieving.

'Have the rains affected anything?' she asked mechanically.

'Only opened up fresh fields for us. The place is a veritable mint, Constance, there's a wealth of multiminerals everywhere. Everything the earth can offer so far, I think, bar oil. Dig a hole and you find something new.'

'You're fortunate,' she commented.

'No.' His answer was so abrupt, so immediate, so final, this time she did turn to look at him. The closed-in expression shocked her. He seemed to have shut a door.

'You have a doctor now?' she said conversationally.

'He's planning our future clinic. We'll need a clinic when we operate full strength.'

'A school?'

'So far that hasn't been considered, since our intake for a few years will comprise only younger couples. Babies are certainly to be expected, but no schoolers yet to be schooled.'

She asked him more questions and he answered them, but she did not ask him the question that was tearing at her to be asked, and she was aware that he knew it. All at once he said without preamble:

'All right, you've done the list, now ask about Yolande.'

'Then – Yolande?' she half-whispered.

'In her room,' he said blankly. 'In a chair.' For a moment he took his eyes off the road and looked at Constance, but what the look said she could not have told.

They did not speak for the rest of the journey.

Quite ridiculously, grieved Constance, sad about the loss of Lorelei, it was fine at Corporation City. How could it be still sunny at seven o'clock in the evening when earlier, only thirty kilometres away, she had lost her little car and everything she had in it?

Anthony Vine drew the waggon up in front of the hotel. The shrubs had grown. The grass was even smoother and greener. There was a squash court now, several tennis courts, a bowling green, a pool.

'You've improved it, if that's possible,' Constance praised. Then she said a little unevenly: 'Oh, the red carpet!'

'Why not?'

'For just me?'

'Couldn't it have been just you before?'

'No, it was for all women, because the only way to keep a man in a place is to keep his woman beside him.' Constance quoted his words a little sharply.

'Well?' he asked keenly.

'Well, your woman is here already, isn't she?' she reminded him almost harshly.

'No, Constance,' he said at once. 'Constance, I want you to understand—'

'I believe I do understand, Mr. Vine. Also I think I regret Lorelei – I mean my little car – very much, because—'

'Yes?'

'Because I could have got Yolande out of here, got her away, and you could have had your promising beginning, your gay start, or whatever it was, after all. Because—' But Constance found she could say no more. She jumped out of the waggon before the porter could come down to help her, and ran up the red carpet, by some miracle not tripping over it since she could see nothing at all for tears, then turned instinctively to the suite that had been allotted to Yolande last time, a lovely set of rooms facing the Territory sunset the same as her suite had, for Territory sunsets were something special, dealing as they did in stunning purples, crimsons and golds, in everything on a grand scale.

She knocked on a door. She heard Yolande's plaintive: 'Oh, Consie, come in.'

Then she opened the door on Yolande at the window, her long flaxen hair shining in the last rays of the sun, her violet eyes courageous above that well-remembered tilted smile. Yolande – in her chair.

'You should have come before.' Yolande released Constance from an embrace that was the first she had ever offered, for she was, as she had often told her fellow worker, strictly a man's woman.

'It wasn't my place. You had friends,' Constance reminded her a little chokily. Yolande's emotional welcome had touched her.

'Not that you'd notice,' said Yolande of the friends.

'You have your mother.'

'My mother would be the last person I'd want here.'

'Mothers are useful,' smiled Constance placatingly, but Yolande would not smile back.

'I wouldn't want her,' she said.

She was studying Constance. 'You look the same, but a bit bedraggled.'

Constance told her about the ill-fated Lorelei, putting much more into it to interest Yolande. But Yolande was not interested.

'Why did you do such a mad thing as bring a car? There are cars laid on. It was even mentioned about fixing one for me to drive, something without foot controls.' She said it almost indifferently. Before Constance could murmur anything tactful, she went on abruptly – and apropos of nothing it seemed:

'How about – him?'

'Him?' echoed Constance.

'Guy?'

'He's in America.'

'How do you know? Did he write to you?'

'He hasn't written, but he told me he was going there.'

'When was that?'

'When the two of us returned to Sydney, but you—' Constance did not finish it.

'And I didn't return with you,' Yolande finished for her. Her voice was quite expressionless. 'All right,' she challenged presently, 'say it. Say you should have come, then none of this would have happened.' Her violet eyes flicked briefly to her legs covered by a thin rug.

Feeling torn to pieces, Constance assured her: 'I won't say it, Yolande.'

'You still can; also I rather wish you'd said it to Guy. That fellow always got the best of a deal, and this would have made it even better.'

'Yolande!' Constance reproached. She repeated: 'I tell you I haven't seen him.'

'Well, not to worry, anyway, I'm not.'

'You're very brave.'

'No, but I'm still the old Yolande, and the big thing … to me … is I'm not disfigured. They're still the same lovely limbs.' Yolande threw off the rug.

They were, Constance saw at a glance, they were slender and shapely as they always had been. 'And yet you can't—' she began, then stopped, distressed.

'And yet I can't walk,' said Yolande for her. 'But not

to worry, as I just said. I'm young, and what you lose on the roundabouts you make up on the swings, or something like that. Wasn't that the rhyme?'

'I don't understand you, Yolande,' sighed Constance.

'You never did, pet, you were always unbelievably naïve. But it's early yet, and given time. . . . Oh, Consie, don't look distressed like that, I do love having you and I'm glad to heaven you came, but I don't want you doleful and going round with a long face, I just want the old Constance. I simply couldn't bear only men around me any more. Fancy me saying that, but it's true.'

'There'll be plenty of women soon. Mr. Vine told me the bungalows are ready.'

'Corporation wives? No, thank you!'

'Yet you yourself one day—' But once more Constance curbed her tongue.

Yolande did not appear to have noticed her slip, or if she did she did not take it from there. She said instead: 'So you lost your car?'

'That's right, and everything in it.'

'Darling, that's terrible. I can help you with lingerie, of course, but when it comes to dresses you're so stunted.' She laughed, the old Yolande bantering laugh.

'Not stunted,' defended Constance, as she always had, because, with astringent Yolande, you continually found you had to, 'just slightly under average, or should I say not arrestingly tall like you.'

Now Yolande grinned impishly. 'Yes, you should say that. Though' . . . her face altering . . . 'little good it did.'

'Yolande—'

'Oh, no, not that, not me and— No, Guy. Honest, Consie, I could have been just a poppy on a tall stem to him.'

'A lovely poppy, and he knew it. All those gowns he designed for you!'

'For his own reward.'

'Well, it was his work, Yolande.'

'Work that certainly never galloped to fame,' yawned Yolande. 'Get off the subject of Guy. He bores me. His dresses bored me. Though I did get a laugh out of your aprony things. Little housewife Consie.'

'You'll be one yourself one day,' Constance reminded her.

'No!'

'But—'

'Perhaps a wife, who knows? but certainly not a house variety. And, as it stands now, not even that.'

'What do you mean, Yolande?'

'Open that second drawer. Help yourself. You'll need nighties as well as undies. And Consie, don't delve. Not yet.'

'Just as you say,' Constance shrugged.

'Then I do say. Because in one minute' . . , peering through the window . . . 'we're having a visitor. Doctor Mason is coming up to see his star patient.'

'Are you?'

'So far I'm his only patient, so I have to be. But no, I believe I would be regardless, with Hugh.'

'Hugh?' queried Constance.

'Hugh Mason. We're that kind of doctor–patient relationship. Open the door, pet.'

Constance moved across the room, did as she was bid. A rather thin, eager, tall young man, dark-eyed, dark-haired, very good-looking, stood waiting to be let in. He smiled at Constance and the smile was warm and sincere. She found it easy to smile back at him.

'Hugh Mason, M.D.,' called Yolande from her chair, and a smile was in her voice as she announced it. As she turned back to the chair with Doctor Mason, Constance saw that Yolande wore a smile in her eyes as well.

Still, that was nothing. Constance thought this as she stood at the window while Hugh Mason took his patient's temperature, held her hand gently but firmly while he checked her pulse. Yolande had always been the same. Travellers in the beautiful silks that Guy had insisted on, departmental heads, buyers, sellers, representatives come to see Guy's collection – Yolande had been through them all. But shouldn't it have been a little different this time, for even though Yolande had tossed back to Constance when Constance had mentioned wives and housewives an eliminating '. . . as it stands now, not even that,' she nonetheless played with a very expensive ring. She did not actually wear it, but she slipped it on and off, estimated its glitter. And it did glitter. It was a very good ring, Constance saw. However, engaged or not engaged, flashing a lovely ring would be typical of Yolande. Constance strongly doubted that even a husband and a string of children would have made any difference to that glorious girl.

Doctor Mason was obviously a very dedicated doctor, a very serious one, but he would have had to

28

have been a not very aware person not to have been conscious now of Yolande's big violet eyes, her long sweeping lashes, her lovely tilted smile . . . all for him. Also not to have been flattered.

'Consie had rotten luck,' Yolande was relating, 'the silly girl brought her car and it was swept off the road by a flash flood. All her things are gone, too, so she'll have to borrow mine. But she's such a tiny town.'

'The bags are here.' Doctor Mason had turned to Constance. 'They arrived just as I did. Evidently Tony sent out for them and they were brought in. There are sure to be some write-offs, but by the look of the cases you could be fortunate. However, your little car—' He spread his thin surgeon's hands in regret.

'Foolish child to have brought it, we have plenty here. Did I tell you, Hugh, that a specially equipped car has been mentioned for me?' Yolande put in.

'Shall you need it?' he smiled.

'That's for you to say,' Yolande smiled back.

'No, it's for you to *do*.'

'Oh, Hugh,' she pouted prettily, and the doctor patted her shoulder.

'I think I'll go down and salvage the wreckage,' said Constance, feeling very much a third person.

'Even if you don't salvage anything you will dine downstairs tonight, Consie? Yes, Hugh, it's actually your difficult patient speaking. I feel I could go down tonight and share a table for four.'

'Four?' the doctor asked.

'Consie, Tony, me . . . you.'

'I was going to spend the evening designing another clinic detail,' Hugh demurred.

'On the first night that I've volunteered to go down?' Yolande reproached.

'But I can put it off, of course.' He smiled at once.

'Then it's all arranged. Consie, go down this minute. If you can't find anything that hasn't been drowned, come back here and we'll see what we can do. Oh, this is going to be fun! Thank you for coming, Consie. Thank you, Hugh.' The big violet eyes with the fanning lashes were lifted to the doctor again, the magic of the uptilted smile was directed on him.

Constance went out of the room. When she went downstairs she was told by the porter that her bags had been dried and taken to her rooms.

'We didn't open them, of course,' he reported, 'but I feel, apart from the outer contents, that you'll probably find them just as they were packed. You're in suite five, Miss Searle.'

Constance went back again up the stairs – the stairs, she thought suddenly and hollowly, that Yolande had fallen down. One day, when delving was permitted, she must ask Yolande all about it. It was better to have everything out in the open.

Suite five was her old suite. She had only slept in it for three nights, but coming back seemed almost like coming home. Constance remembered that first time when Anthony Vine had led her into it, then beckoned her, before she could look around, to the window. He had pointed to the west, that fabulous purple, crimson, golden west of inside Australia, and then he had spoken excitingly, exciting to Constance, about this strange, newly abundant place.

'Once, it was dismissed as desert, barren country,

gibber country, yet now it comprises some of the richest acres in the world. I'll take you out and show you the red flags marching to kingdom come, or so it seems, but they do, of course, eventually stop, and they comprise the grid line for our geos on the job. It's wonderful out there, all yellow, ochre and sienna, it's moon country that no one really believes.' He had dreamed a moment, she recalled. 'Burning hot by day, sometimes cold as charity at night, rough, tough, ruthless, yet still giving. It's given to me.' He had turned and looked at her with those deep blue eyes in the leather brown face, the weather-hardened face of a man who has spent most of his life in places other men only read and dream about, a man who has found his pot of gold not at the end of a rainbow but in country where the colours come richer than any rainbow and in country that gives more than a pot of gold.

But now the yellow, ochre and sienna were gone, the moon world had become a blossoming garden. There were still riches for the taking, for Anthony Vine had said: 'Dig a hole and you find something.' But that seemed the only similarity from the last time she was here.

Constance turned back from the window to tackle her bags. The only similarity, she thought bitterly again.

'I'm sure Yolande will help out,' he had tossed when she believed she had lost the bags. 'After all, she has little need herself.'

Also— 'No,' he had answered when she had said: 'Your woman is here already.' Later he had told her: 'I want you to understand—'

31

CHAPTER THREE

ALL the contents of the suitcases were in good order, even the garments on the outer side were unaffected. Either the flood had been so brief it had had no time to deposit its murky evidence or the bags had been stout ones. Constance looked happily at her clothes, feeling that this, so far, was her first piece of good luck. She shouldn't say that really, since she was here, alive and safe, but everything was so much different to what she had thought it would be, even though she had allowed a few doubts. Anthony Vine was different.

She took out her clothes, shook them, then placed them on hangers. So much nicer to have your own garments than borrow, she thought, for although Yolande was generous, she would also have laughed as she had pressed her generosity on Constance, she would have made those bantering, patronizing remarks about 'stunted' and 'tiny town'. For that was Yolande.

Well, thought Constance tolerantly, laughter never hurt anyone. She selected a garment and held it up against her, then regarded herself in the mirror. We can't, her thoughts ran on, all be models. I modelled, yes, but I was never a model. She smiled at the idea, as Yolande always had smiled.

Constance studied herself frankly in the reflecting glass. A smallish girl. A bluntish girl as to features and short-cropped, thick brown hair. Nothing fair and ethereal, nothing exquisitely chiselled, no elegant aristocratic look as with Yolande, no arresting height, no arresting anything, really, and that had pleased Guy considerably.

'A housewife going shopping never steps out of *Vogue*,' he had declared with satisfaction. 'You are just perfect for what I have in mind, Worm.' He had called Constance quite fondly Worm. 'A nice little homebody. One of those thrifty little souls checking first on the price before she buys. A neat little baggage. Brushed locks, scrubbed face, turned-up nose. You're just what the designer of bread-and-butter offerings could order, my dear Consie.'

'No jam on the bread-and-butter?' she remembered sighing.

'Leave jam to Yolande,' he had grinned.

Well, if she was no glamour girl, the gown she held up was certainly nonetheless very lovely. It should be. It carried a very telling tag, telling to the discerning: 'By Guy.'

Guy had given it to her, and though it was not slinky, and breathless, and head-turning, it was still a darling dress, and she was glad it was not damaged. I'll wear it, she decided.

She showered in her private annexe. Pale yellow décor here, pale yellow towels, pale yellow curtains, even pale yellow soap. No, Mr. Anthony Vine had not forgotten anything, except—

Except pity, Constance thought. Except – love.

When she came out of the shower, she went to the table and picked up the phone. The voice that answered was male, for the female side of Corporation had still not arrived. Probably they would come, along with the Corporation wives, next week. She asked for Yolande's room.

She gave Yolande time to steer her wheelchair across her suite, the realization that she must do this sending Constance's nails cutting into her palms.

'Yes?' asked Yolande.

'Me, dear. Constance. My things are all right.'

'Oh, good, then you won't be borrowing?'

'No.'

'But you will be coming down to dinner?'

'Only if you're going.'

'It's because of you that I am. Consie, I feel renewed somehow. If anyone had told me a woman could do that to me . . .' A low amused laugh. 'What are you wearing?'

'One of Guy's.'

'Oh.'

'Well, I couldn't wear better, could I?'

'That's a matter of opinion,' drawled Yolande.

'Also I have nothing else.'

'Then, darling, wear it by all means. Dinner is at eight. Tap on my door. Oh, Consie, it's really going to be fun!'

Constance heard the phone go down and she thought: How can she? How can she be so brave?

She began to dress. It seemed a long time since she had slipped into floor-length chiffon, into satin pumps. Since she had left Guy and joined the typing pool it had been a strictly business world for her. She had made no new male acquaintances, nor wanted to. Just work through the day, then the girls' company after work, and a movie or a gallery at the week-end had sufficed.

But now she found herself enjoying it all. Guy had wonderful talent, he must have more than his share to make something out of the housebody he, and she, considered Constance Searle to be. She looked at her reflection in the mirror. Blue, naturally. 'A girl-next-door like you,' Guy had said, 'simply must wear blue.' But it was still a very beautiful blue, a vibrant cornflower, and it had a lovely cut. Constance even found herself swirling round, something she had not done since her dancing days.

She picked up a fluffy stole and went down the passage to tap on Yolande's door.

It was like coming painfully to earth again to see Yolande in her chair. In her own absorption she had forgotten all about Yolande's chair. But the confining chair was the only confining thing about Yolande, she found at once. The girl looked lovelier than Constance had ever seen her look, and that was saying everything, for every time you looked at Yolande you looked at something even lovelier than before.

'Oh, Yolande!' she breathed.

Yolande, well pleased with her effect on Constance, smiled: 'You're quite an eyeful yourself, pet. Guy's so-called magic, I suppose.'

'Yes.'

'He could design when he felt like it, I must admit that,' Yolande said grudgingly. 'As a matter of fact this is one of his, too. Certainly not intended to be modelled as I'm modelling it now, but effective?'

'You know you look a dream,' Constance came back.

'Hugh is coming up to help manoeuvre me downstairs. It will be quite a job, I expect.'

'You haven't been before?'

'Since it happened I've eaten up here. But tonight it's different. You have come. Also, there are quite a few men eating there now. I'm told. The executive staff, the department bosses. If I don't go now, their wives will be here, and men accompanied with their wives are dreary affairs.' She laughed. 'I can hear footsteps. That will be Hugh now.'

It was the doctor, immaculate in dinner-suit, but he was not alone.

'Two penguins!' Yolande clapped her slender white hands.

'It's an important occasion, Yolande.' Anthony Vine came forward with a smile and a bow. He did not look at Constance.

Hugh, meanwhile, was manipulating the wheelchair backwards and forwards, evidently estimating its passage through the door, down the hall, then down the stairs.

'No.' Anthony Vine said it casually and genially enough, but he said it firmly. Stepping forward, he leaned over Yolande, lifted her bodily, then turned to the door.

Hugh, seeing his purpose, had hurried across to open the door, to check the corridor and stairs to make sure that everything was clear. It was clear, and Anthony Vine strode arrogantly forward with his beautiful burden. Hugh was still ahead clearing the way, getting a chair ready.

Constance came slowly, silently, behind. But at the threshold of the dining-room she stopped feeling oddly left out and instead caught her breath. The room was quite beautiful. It had not had its chandeliers before, its floor-length drapes, its thick lush carpet. Also, as well as the ceiling lights, there were now hundreds of candles, candles on tables, in quiet corners, in secluded nooks. They soaked up the shadows most successfully, yet gently, provocatively as well. A romantic semi-light remained.

Anthony Vine carried Yolande to the table he had selected, then he put her gently down on a waiting chair. It was the first gentleness he had shown the girl, Constance thought, for although she had not heard him in actual conversation with Yolande, he had had conversation about Yolande with Constance, and his conversation there, she considered, had been anything but gentle. She found herself withdrawing, resenting his outward show of concern. Resenting, though she would not have admitted it, his fingers on Yolande's lovely white arms.

'I think we'll put you here, Miss Searle,' she heard him saying. What had happened to his: '... for heaven's sake, not Mr. Vine. Not up here, Constance.'

'Thank you, Mr. Vine,' Constance answered stiffly.

There had only been a skeleton staff before, now the room was full of uniformed waiters.

Diners, too, were actually arriving. All male at this stage, but in a week or so, Anthony Vine was telling them, they would be bringing their wives. Yolande made a little grimace.

'Not every night, though,' Anthony smiled at her,

'just special occasions or week-ends. I'm a great believer in family living. That's why I've gone to such trouble with the bungalows.' Another little grimace from Yolande.

'Well, my butterfly,' Anthony said tolerantly to Yolande, 'that is how I want it. What does our Miss Searle think?'

His question took Constance by surprise. Although she shared the table she had felt apart from the others. Now she tried to gather her wits.

'Consie is an aprony female,' said Yolande in her rather pouting but fascinating voice. 'She would love a family bungalow. She would think it out of this world.'

'Then we're depriving her here in a luxury hotel?' Anthony Vine said with mock concern.

'No deprivation when it's only for such a short time.' Constance found her tongue at last.

An orchestra had started to play. It was not a large band but it was a good one, Constance noted. She sipped the very excellent wine that she had been poured and eventually felt herself relaxing.

The conversation naturally enough centred around Corporation and future Corporation activities; also, since the doctor was present, the clinic that was soon to open. There would be a great deal of the clinic space allotted to Casualty, Hugh Mason explained, for in a project like this, one had to expect a rather high accident rate.

'But,' Doctor Hugh smiled, 'we already have a maternity ward, and that, I think, is quite unique for an undertaking that's barely begun.'

'Yes.' Anthony Vine took up the story. 'One of our up-and-coming engineers could only be inveigled here on the promise that his very pregnant young wife would get as good or better treatment as in a big city.'

'Couldn't you have signed up another engineer?' came in Yolande, patently bored.

'Andrew and Sandra Javes were manna from heaven,' said Anthony Vine. 'They were what I wanted: a beginning. I wanted to drive it very emphatically to Corporation City that here was no place from which to line your pockets, then promptly retreat. I wanted C.C. to be known as something enduring, something intrinsic.'

'Known as home,' Constance heard herself say, and flushed. She did not look at Anthony. She felt annoyed with herself that she had spoken.

'It all depends,' sneered Yolande, 'on what home was like.' She glanced around her, very aware that she was the cynosure of all eyes. She would have been, anyway, carried in helpless and appealing as she had been, but when the pity passed, and the men looked again and saw how angelically lovely she was, then the focus would become a brilliant specialized spotlight. Yolande clearly was anticipating that.

But she did not enjoy Anthony Vine's next words.

'We have an excellent Sister coming up, capable, so Hugh assures me, of organizing then supervising both casualty and maternity. Hugh served at Martha General at the same time as Sister, then Nurse, Cressida Moore, and he's most enthusiastic.'

'Can one woman do both those things herself?' doubted Yolande. 'Casualty and maternity?'

'She will organize, then direct their functioning,' explained Hugh. 'Naturally she'll have a staff.'

'For both accidents and babies.' Yolande had forgotten her spotlight and was now not looking so angelic. 'What about general cases?'

'Naturally those too.'

'And cripples?' There was a tight note now in Yolande's voice and Constance saw the two men exchange quick looks.

'Darling,' she said, leaning across the table to Yolande, 'if you'd like to go upstairs—'

'She doesn't wish to go upstairs,' Anthony Vine came in quietly but finally. 'She's going to have some more wine, some special strawberries our chef has had flown up for the occasion when la belle Yolande finally has graced our table and which he has appropriately named Strawberry Yolande, and she's going to continue enjoying the admiring glances of our fellow diners.' He looked across at Yolande.

The doctor had put a comforting hand over Yolande's hand, everyone in the room looked either sympathetic or adoring, and without much effort Yolande became an angel again. She hung her head in a little-girl gesture and said: 'Please forgive.'

Everyone loved her.

Well, that was Yolande, Constance thought soon afterwards, enjoying la belle Yolande's brandy and sugar-drenched strawberries at the same time as la belle Yolande's sugar-drenched smile. Sweet when she wanted to be. Not sweet when she was in a mood. But she had every right to such moods, Constance's thoughts went on, to be so young and so beautiful and

41

so hopeless. She gave a little shiver.

'The air-conditioning is a little chill for you?' Anthony Vine asked as he found the stole she had brought with her and placed it around her shoulders.

'No, it's quite perfect.' As everything, outwardly, is perfect in this ordered place, Constance thought.

'Yet you flinched.'

'Someone walking over my grave.' Constance tried to be patronizingly facetious.

'But I think it was not a flinch for the future but rather a flinch for now.'

'How ridiculous! Yet perhaps you're right, perhaps it is a little cool.' The easiest way to get rid of this man was to agree with him, she decided.

'Then we must alter the temperature.'

'No . . . no, I may be the only one finding it cool.'

'We must still alter it.'

'Don't fuss, Mr. Vine!' Constance snapped. She did not feel up to being co-operative any longer.

He looked at her thoughtfully, then nodded. 'Yes, I expect there's reason in what you say. Why should the degree of heat or cool be altered for one person only, wouldn't it be simpler to alter that person's own heat or cool?'

'I don't understand, Mr. Vine.'

'Miss Searle, will you dance?'

. . . Will you dance? Constance could not believe she had heard aright. She sat staring incredulously at the man, this man who already had excused himself to the helpless girl beside him and actually risen to bow formally to Constance.

'Will you dance?' he said again.

'You're not being funny,' she said in a low voice for him alone.

'It was not my intention.'

'You're acting in shocking, unbelievably shocking bad taste.' Constance found she could say it, since the orchestra, caught up in a popular number, was louder than it had been. Doctor Mason, too, had Yolande fully absorbed in something he was telling her.

'Will you dance, Miss Searle?' Anthony Vine asked a third time. 'Please to answer yes or no, because you, not Yolande this time, are now inviting the looks. Also, I'm beginning to feel a fool standing here.'

'Then sit down ... go out ... do anything you wish.'

'I wish to dance with you. I danced, you might remember, another time. We matched quite well.'

Everything matched then, thought Constance, a kindly man had matched with a believing girl. But now the man's kindness had turned to hardness, and a girl's belief had gone.

'If you don't get up in one second,' Anthony Vine was saying, close now to Constance's ear, '*you* are going to be the fool.'

'How can you ask such a thing of me ... how can you ...'

'Yolande is smiling at us. She's tapping her fingers in time to the rhythm. She's giving her audience big sad looks to remind them that once upon a time she, too, was asked to dance.'

'You're a sadist!' she snapped.

'Perhaps, but still glance across at Yolande and see for yourself, see that she's revelling in all this.'

43

Constance glanced, and saw that he was right. Yolande was looking beautiful and regretful and unselfish all in the one sweet trembling movement of her tilted lips. The girl caught Constance's eyes and flicked her own in agreement. Dance, the flick said.

Not believing it all was happening, not crediting that such a thing could happen, Constance rose and allowed herself to be enfolded in Anthony Vine's arms. At once, as if by a signal ... *had* someone signalled? ... the chandeliers were switched off so that they moved only in candlelight.

The music swelled, then diminished to a soft rhythm.

As if one person, not two, for Anthony Vine had been right, they had matched well, they moved round the room.

For all her cold anger, her dismay, Constance was still sharply conscious of the closeness of the man, just as she had been that other time they had danced. But there had been the beginnings of a sweet response in her then, not a hard reluctant but somehow *compelled* interest as she found in herself now. What had happened (besides the closing of a chapter for Yolande) to Anthony Vine when Yolande had fallen down a flight of stairs?

They danced wordlessly, outwardly perfectly, but Constance knew, and she knew that Anthony knew, that though they were breath-close, they were still a smile apart.

'Thank you, Miss Searle.' Anthony Vine turned and applauded the orchestra. 'I think I'll let you do what you wanted to now,' he said, 'and that is take Yolande upstairs. After all, it's enough for a first time.' He preceded Constance back to the table.

Yolande was willing to go. The other diners were getting ready to leave, and though she had enjoyed their sympathetic looks, she had not enjoyed the dancing. For a little apron-girl, Consie performed far too well. She smiled ruefully, sweetly and wistfully, though, and looked pleased when the doctor this time, and not Anthony, carried her up the stairs.

Constance and Anthony came some steps behind them, Anthony watching Hugh to see if he wearied, for he was a slimmer build of man and Yolande was a tall girl.

At the turn of the flight, Constance paused a moment then half spoke, half whispered: 'It was down these stairs that she—'

'Yes.' The answer was terse, quite unadorned.

'I must ask her,' Constance said dully.

'It would be better if you got her to show you.'

'Show me?'

'That's what I said.'

'Mr. Vine, I don't understand you,' she sighed.

'And it wouldn't occur to you to try.'

'Try what?'

'Understand.'

'I don't understand that, either.'

'Then leave it, Miss Searle.' They had reached the upper flight by now. 'Our patient has evidently arrived safely. In which case I won't proceed any further. Good night. Thank you for the dance.' He wheeled round and went down the stairs leaving Constance standing there.

It was a few minutes before she could bring herself to

proceed along the corridor to Yolande's suite. The doctor was just leaving.

'You did wonderfully tonight, Yolande,' Constance heard him commend the girl. 'I was proud of you.'

'I did it for you, Hugh.'

'Then try some more, please. Try to get up, Yolande, and move across the room.'

'Without your help?' The fright in Yolande's voice was too sharp, too real for incredulity. Quickly Constance stepped into the suite and said:

'Darling, I'm here. I'll help. It's what I came for.'

She looked at Hugh, half expecting to find that same enigmatical look that Anthony had worn, but the doctor looked warmly, sympathetically back at Constance.

'You do that, Constance. She needs every help we can give her. Good night, my dear. You've been a grand girl.' He leaned over and kissed her brow lightly, then he went.

Constance crossed to Yolande. 'All that goes for me, too,' she said sincerely. 'You were very, very brave.'

'But very, very imprisoned.' For the first time since she had returned here Constance heard a despairing note in Yolande's voice. It was all Constance needed. For a brief ... a very brief ... period, in Anthony's presence, she had actually wondered about Yolande, whether she – if she— But now she felt sure. Anyway, hadn't Doctor Mason just said: 'She needs every help we can give her.' He had not said: 'Don't ask her, get her to show you,' as Anthony Vine had done.

'Oh, Yolande!' Constance went tenderly to her. She helped the girl into bed, sat by her until she heard the even breathing telling her that Yolande was asleep. Then she tiptoed out to her own suite.

She did not go to bed herself for over an hour. She stood at the window looking out on a velvet night, for nights never came more deeply velvet than Centre nights. The stars, too, blossomed, no pinpoints of silver here but great splashy flowers of light you felt you could reach up to and pluck.

It was all incredibly beautiful, but Constance, in spite of her awareness, missed most of the beauty. How could she see with tears pricking her eyes?

Tears for Yolande. What would happen to Yolande? But tears, too, she knew, and despised herself for that knowledge, for something ... some*one* ... else. For a man who had changed so much she felt she did not know him any more. For Anthony Vine, stranger.

CHAPTER FOUR

CONSTANCE woke at seven. Apart from week-ends, she had been waking for years at seven. Seven had given her the necessary time for a shower and breakfast at not too hectic a pace before she left for the office. First Guy's office, then the various offices supplied by the typing pool. It seemed luxurious now not to leap up at once and grab the bathroom before someone else beat her to it. She glanced smugly in the direction of her own private pale yellow bath annexe and at the same time rejoiced in the fact that even when Yolande had been the old complete Yolande the girl never had been punctual, never beaten her to a morning appearance, which all meant that Constance could lie abed now with a clear conscience.

She did not lie long, though. A scatter of little pebbles on her window brought her to the window in a hurry. Who on earth— She looked down and saw Anthony Vine. The idea of the owner of a super hotel standing beneath a window and throwing up pebbles to attract attention was so laughable that in spite of herself Constance laughed.

The man grinned back, and for a moment Constance felt there had been no winds of change after all, that he was not a stranger.

'Look,' he called, and waved an arm.

Constance looked, gasped, then cried out: 'Lorelei!'

'Rescued from a ditch and towed in. Certainly

not A1, but possibly able to be repaired. Come down.'

'I'm just up, I haven't dressed, I haven't showered.'

'Do you dress for a shower?' he asked. 'Put on a gown or a wrap or a towel or something, but come. Surely your old girl deserves that.'

For answer Constance grabbed the only robe she had brought, a short Chinese happy coat, and ran out and down. Once out of the hotel she hurried round to the courtyard where Anthony and Lorelei waited. 'Oh, Lorelei!' she greeted, and patted the Mini's muddy bonnet.

'Like you,' teased Anthony Vine, looking at her morning face, 'she'll come up better after a scrub.'

'Am I that cold-creamy?'

'You're rosy from slumber,' he said in mock flattery, 'but don't get carried away, you also have sleep in your eyes.' But he did not take his own eyes away from those eyes.

'Thank you for bringing her in,' Constance said.

'To leave her out there would be a kind of pollution.'

'Yes, it is awful to see cars strewn around. You really think she'll mend?'

'My word was "possibly". Meanwhile until Jim gives a verdict you must take the second Holden.'

'No.'

'I'm not inviting you, Miss Searle, I'm telling you. I have a lot of chores lined up for you, each located in a different office, and in a place like C.C., where different offices can sometimes be up to a mile apart, a car is not a luxury, it's a must.'

'But I don't understand. I'm here for Yolande.'

'I thought you could take Yolande with you

'Yes, I would want to, but – but I'm not actually working for you, am I?'

'That,' said Anthony Vine, 'is something you and I have to discuss. No, not here. We may be in the middle of nowhere, but it is still not quite the thing to sign up a young lady still wearing her short pyjamas.'

'I'm sorry, but you did say to come.'

'I'm not complaining.' His blue eyes flicked briefly down the brief happy coat to Constance's slim bare legs. 'Run up and dress, eat the breakfast I'll have sent up, then meet me here and we'll try you out on the Holden.'

'No need – I mean, if I do agree to what you ask, I've driven for years.'

'Your Mini is a manual, this is an automatic – you have driven automatics?'

'Well – no.'

'Run up,' he said, and turned away before she could think of anything else to say. After a vexed pause, Constance obeyed.

After her shower she zipped up a short, pink sleeveless shift, for there was one thing you could always be certain of here in the Territory: the days would be warm to hot. The nights, too, more often than not, though occasionally a sharp breath could blow, but the days were like the matched tears in a long amber necklace, full and golden and dropping slow.

When she came out of the bath annexe she found a tray on the little table. Iced fruit, cereal, an omelette and toast and honey. A large pot of steaming coffee. Much better, she thought, than a bowl of muesli while you watched the clock, but there had to be a catch somewhere. Admittedly Anthony Vine had asked her here, he had written 'Come', but that had been to see Yolande, and she had seen her, so what happened now?

A second scatter of pebbles cut short any conjecture. Constance went to the window and called down:

'That's undignified. Aren't you aware that you're the boss?'

'So long as *you* are aware of it,' he called back. He moved across to the Holden that now stood where the Mini had stood ... Lorelei must have been towed away ... and beckoned her down.

'I wanted to peep in on Yolande,' said Constance rather crossly as she joined him in the courtyard.

'It would be a waste of time, she doesn't stir until eleven.'

That could be true. Yolande had never appeared at Guy's before noon. But the positive way Anthony Vine said it left Constance no doubt that he knew Yolande's waking time right to the minute. Personally knew it.

'True,' he agreed, reading her thoughts, 'and she really does wake up rosy from slumber.'

'Sleep in her eyes?'

'Her violet eyes,' he concurred. He nodded Constance into the passenger's seat of the Holden. 'I'll let you try her when we're further out,' he said.

'There's no need,' she protested.

'A lot of need. Manuals and automatics—'

'I meant I wouldn't be driving.'

'Then what the hell will you be doing?' he asked.

They had moved away from the centre by now, and Constance tried to recognize the flowering paradise from the barren waste she remembered last time. It was not easy. The gravelly track that had wound through moon country with the golden bars of sun hitting the windscreen to add any relief was changed to a vast coloured garden, mostly Salvation Jane, a lilac-blue screen of Jane wherever you turned.

Also a lagoon had happened since last time. A large sparkling stretch of water with insects weaving gauzy patterns over it, with frogs croaking in a busy chorus.

'Last appearance, so the natives have told me,' Anthony Vine said of the lagoon, 'some fifty years ago. It will probably be another fifty years for a second performance.'

'But still the minerals go on?'

'They're unchanged. Among the other few things unchanged' . . . he gave her a quick oblique look . . . 'is the artesian pool. Remember that?'

'Oh, yes.' She remembered it clearly and with pleasure. Some ten miles from C.C. she had been shown a sky blue circle of smiling water. It had had ribbons of steam rising from it. The bore had been delightfully heated from its subterranean source, and Constance, dabbling her fingers into it, had announced that she preferred this offering of nature to the hotel's luxury pool.

'What, no tiles?' Anthony had laughed at the time. 'No changing rooms?'

'Artesian water is supposed to be good for rheumatism,' she had proffered.

'You don't know what the word means. You two girls are the ungirt runners in the poem' ... Yolande had been there as well ... 'you swing ungirded hips ... the rain is on your lips.'

'Rain up here?'

'It comes.'

It had come, thought Constance now. And one of the runners did not run any more. She tried not to let him see her shiver this time, but he still must have, for he said:

'And that, too, is changed.' But he did not go on with it. He pulled up the car, got out, then beckoned her to the driver's seat.

'Why?' she asked.

'You don't generally drive from where you're sitting now.'

'I—'

'All right, Miss Searle.' He got back in the car again and took out the makings of a cigarette – he had always rolled his own, and it always had fascinated her. That dry whisper of tobacco in a big brown palm, that meticulous packing of the flattened weed. That final licking of the edges together.

He lit the finished article, smoked a moment, then said:

'Because.'

'Because?' she queried.

'Because I need you in my employ.'

'You didn't say so in your letter.'

'No, I said Come. I' ... hesitantly ... 'couldn't trust myself with more.'

'What do you mean, Mr. Vine?'

'But now it's different. What I had in mind is changed, just as the rest is changed.'

'Except the artesian pool.'

He shrugged, then went on.

'I had thought you might achieve something with Yolande,' he said.

'If you're thinking differently now I must say you haven't given me much time.'

'Agreed, but the end result, I believe, will still be the same. No, you are not the answer there, Miss Searle.'

Constance sat silent. She was angry that he could reach a decision so quickly . . . she was also angry at the hollowness in her. When she had read that 'Come' that had comprised his letter to her in Sydney as well as pertaining to Yolande she had thought—

'Please go on, Mr. Vine,' she said.

'Although you're not the answer, you'll still be good for Yolande, if not perhaps in the way I hoped.'

'Then—?'

'Then I suggest you work for me, at least for C.C., besides being a companion to Yolande. Yes, I know she wrote and asked you, just as I asked you, but I also know Yolande and how she can blow hot, then cold. Tomorrow' . . . another shrug . . . 'she could want you out instead.'

'Then I would certainly leave.'

'That would be inadvisable for Yolande. It would also be a loss for C.C. We badly need a woman here to help with our initial female intake, and I can think of no one more suitable than you.'

'Thank you. What qualities were you looking for?' Constance spoke stiffly.

'Serenity. Resourcefulness. Judgment.' A pause. 'Lack of competition.'

'I think you mean by that last someone not to raise envy.'

He looked at her. He saw thick shining brown hair springing from a wide brow, a sweet curved mouth, a small, very firm but somehow vulnerable chin.

'Perhaps.' He said it a little gruffly, but she did not notice. She was busy considering.

'I would sooner work for my keep than be a visitor,' she admitted.

'Then I offer you this job of ombudsman ... or should it be ombudswoman?'

'Just tell me what would be expected of me.'

'Friendship with the wives, which should come easily to you.'

'Because of my lack of competition?'

He ignored her. 'A general getting-to-know-you, getting them all to know each other. Help in settling in. There'll be sure to be some who will look beyond the luxury hotel I've so shrewdly provided to the empty desert beyond.'

'The *flowering* desert.'

'But still empty and lonely and hundreds of miles from home. You will start pottery classes, drama classes, yoga, eurythmics, tango lessons.'

'Whether I can dance or not?'

'You can dance,' he said remindingly. 'At times you'll just talk, or you'll just keep silent, or make a cup of tea, or take a cup of tea. Well?'

'For which I stay at the hotel?'

'And receive a salary.'

'You're generous.'

'We pay generously for good service.'

'I'll try to earn my remuneration,' she said, poker-faced.

'Then you agree?'

'Yes.'

'Good. First of all, pending the repair of your car, this car is yours, Miss Searle. So now will you kindly change seats.'

Constance did so, and because she always had loved driving, always had had a liking for anything mechanical, she picked up the points quickly.

'I pass you,' he said at length. 'Will you now drive me back to the hotel in your car.'

Constance did so, rather pleased that she had caught on so quickly, that she was driving so efficiently.

'Yolande said something,' she said conversationally, 'about you fixing a special control car for her.'

He did not answer.

'I know they're made,' she went on, 'and I'm sure that Yolande—'

He moved slightly in the passenger's seat beside her. 'Then don't be sure,' he advised coolly.

'But you said—'

'I didn't say.'

'Yolande told me that you—'

'Yolande has these hallucinations.'

'You mean it isn't true?'

'Only in her thoughts.'

'And you mean – you wouldn't?'

'Yes, I mean just that. I didn't say such a thing and I wouldn't do it. Well' ... his voice rising ... 'what are

56

you going to do about it? Decide against the job after all?'

'No. On the contrary. I know now that I should be here.' Constance's voice, too, had risen.

'To stop an imposition ... or is that too weak a word?'

'Mr. Vine, it's not my place to interfere.'

'Quite right.'

'But to tell a helpless girl—'

'I did not tell her. Good lord, why should I? Why should I encourage someone to continue the way she's going when there's no reason for her to be that way at all?'

'What – what do you mean?' stammered Constance.

'I mean there's nothing wrong with her.'

'Except a simple matter of being unable to walk.'

'I wish to God it was simple. It's not. But involved or not, one thing remains, Miss Searle. There's nothing on earth to stop Yolande from getting to her feet and walking. Don't look at me like that. Don't you think I *know*? I've flown every specialist worth his salt up here. I've even inveigled one from the States. And the verdict? Nothing. Nothing at all. Yet Yolande can't walk. You're still looking incredulously at me. All right, ask Hugh. He's been in all this as long as I have, in fact it was Hugh ...' His voice trailed off.

'Yes, ask Mason, Miss Searle,' he advised. 'Also stop the car and put me off at that next building. I think I've had enough.'

'*You've* had enough!' But Constance still stopped the car where he told her.

He got off without another word, and she continued along the track to the hotel.

She left the car in the courtyard and ran up the stairs to go to her suite, but half-way along the passage she changed her mind and tapped instead on Yolande's door.

'Come in, Consie,' Yolande called.

The girl was still in bed, and only just awake, by her drowsy look. She was also, Constance noted, 'rosy with slumber', as Anthony Vine had said, though with sleep in her eyes. But violet eyes. That made a big difference.

Constance crossed the room and sat on Yolande's bed. How beautiful she was. How could she be resentful that Yolande woke up in a way Constance was sure she never could! How could any man – how could he—

'So serious,' pouted Yolande. 'I brought you up here for smiles.'

'Then I have one. We have a car.'

'I had that at my disposal any time.'

'But not with me driving it. Where do you wish to go, madam?'

Yolande was pleased. 'Oh, good, we'll do a lot of things I'd planned.'

'After I do the things Mr. Vine has planned,' Constance warned. 'Primarily I'm in his employ.'

'It's the least he can do,' Yolande uncharitably replied.

'Is it, Yolande? I mean should you say that, dear? Does Mr. Vine really owe you – I mean us – anything?'

'Me? Yes – he owes me two legs.' A pause. 'And a ring.'

'Yolande—'

'Well, I fell down his stairs, didn't I?'

'But a ring? You have a beautiful ring.'

'Yet for which finger of which hand?'

There was a silence. Constance broke it. 'Darling, do you want to tell me?' she half-whispered.

'No.'

'But if I knew—'

'No. For heaven's sake *no*, Consie.' Another pause. 'Sorry, pet, but lying like this you do get to the end of everything.'

Carefully Constance probed: 'But do you *have* to, Yolande?'

'Lie here, you mean? Or sit in a chair?'

'Yes. Oh, I'm sorry, Yolande.'

Now the pause was a long one. Then: 'Yes, I do,' said Yolande. 'I know what you're driving at, Consie, I know what you're thinking.'

'Not thinking, just – wondering.'

'Then wonder, but let me assure you that I can't walk, Constance; *I can't walk.*' The girl looked up at Constance, and though truth had never been a favourite commodity of Yolande's, Constance saw truth there.

'Dear Yolande,' she soothed, and kissed her. 'Look, I won't delve. Instead I'll take you out. Have you had breakfast?'

'I always skip it. Lying around can encourage a spread, and one day . . . one never knows . . .'

'Yolande, *I* know. You're going to be whole again. You *are*. But you should still eat something. Shall I ask the kitchen for a flask and hamper?'

'Yes, do that, a picnic would be fun. But first bring

over those clothes.'

'You can manage?'

'Very well. In fact I'm quite expert. It's only the other end of me that's the snag.' Yolande gave a comical shrug. 'Get along with you, Consie, and see to that hamper.'

Laughing, though she should have felt like tears, Constance thought, she went down to the kitchen.

With Yolande propped up with cushions beside her, Constance first of all familiarized herself with Corporation City. She went in and out of the 'streets', past the bungalows, past the bachelor chalets, drove round the new golf course, the bowling green, the sports arena, the hospital. Only at the hospital did Yolande evince any interest.

'I hope Hugh has spent some of the money Anthony allowed him on himself,' she said. 'It would be just like that dear foolish thing to forgo a carpet for an extra piece of equipment. Blow the horn, Consie, I want to see Hugh, but I don't want to try to manoeuvre myself out to do it.'

'You brought your sticks, didn't you, Yolande? Wouldn't it be better if you made an effort on your own account? I mean, dear, they do say—'

'Oh, not you now!' Yolande's tilted smile went down like a reversed horseshoe. 'Yolande, do try ... Yolande, make an effort ... Yolande, it's all in the mind. I'd just like to see them in my place!'

'Darling, I'm sorry. I didn't mean it. It's simply that I get stiff myself, if I sit too long, so I thought you—'

'Then stop thinking, Consie, and fetch Hugh.' A little fond smile. 'Dear Hugh!'

Constance got out and walked into the clinic.

The hospital proved all that hospitals should be, white walls, brown floors, that familiar and somehow reassuring smell of polish, hygiene, antiseptic, that air of getting better. That, anyway, was what Constance said to Hugh.

'Yes. But I'm afraid Yolande will be disappointed when she sees it. Not with the wards but the consulting room – she had visions of cedar desks and thick carpet.'

'Which you spent on an extra cot,' smiled Constance. 'I have our girl with me now. She's in the Holden Mr. Vine has allotted me.'

'Then I'll come out, of course.'

Constance paused. 'I was hoping she'd come in to you.'

'It's asking a lot. It's not easy even for an agile person to leap in and out of a car.'

'And Yolande isn't agile, is she?' asked Constance.

The doctor looked quickly at her. 'You can see that for yourself.'

'But not medically. I'd like a medico's opinion, please, Hugh. I've already had a Corporation boss's.'

Hugh sighed. 'I was rather expecting this.'

'Then?'

There was an estimating silence for a few moments. 'Tell me first what Tony Vine said,' Hugh stipulated.

'Among other things that he didn't intend to encourage someone to continue the way she was going when there was no reason for her to be that way at all. Then he backed it up with an account of specialists . . .

61

even one from the States. He told me their verdict. True or not true, Hugh?'

'True, Constance.'

'Then?'

'Then *what*? Oh, damn it, Constance, what do you really want from me?'

'I want Hugh's version.'

'After an American top-notcher's?'

'Yes. You see, he just examined Yolande, then left, but you've been here at Corporation City with her now for weeks . . . ever since it happened.'

'That's correct,' he agreed.

'Then what have you found?'

Another pause – it was a morning of estimating pauses – then: 'What they found, of course. What Anthony Vine finds. But—'

'But?'

'I see it differently. I see a girl who should be able to walk but can't very differently from Anthony, Constance. Were my fellow doctors here with me, they would say the same. You see, in medicine there's no simple black and white, there's a very large gamut of colours. Most important of all, there are many varieties of patients. Some will make light of things that gravely matter; some will complain bitterly of nothing at all. But we can't judge them on it, since the nothing-at-alls can quite feasibly feel as legitimate a pain as the true sufferers. It's not their fault they're built like that.'

'And you think Yolande—'

'Yes . . . yet not entirely. I believe Yolande wants very badly to be better, but she simply can't make herself. She can't because the impetus is missing, she has to have an inspiration, an urge.'

'Surely Anthony Vine—' began Constance. After all, even though nothing seemed to have eventuated, Yolande had stopped back for Anthony, and as far as she knew Anthony Vine had not protested.

'No.' Hugh shook his head.

'Then—' But Constance did not finish what she started to say. If Hugh did not know how Yolande obviously felt about him, it was not her business to tell him, unless, of course, it could bring about that miracle for Yolande. She moistened her lips.

But the doctor spoke before she could. 'We, Vine and myself, believed you might help Yolande.'

'A woman?' Constance said wryly, and he nodded wryly back.

'We even thought Yolande might feel a jealous urge when she saw you getting around.'

'You chose a wrong subject, Hugh. As Mr. Vine told me earlier today, I'm one of those comfortable types offering no competition.'

'That I would not believe, Constance.' The doctor smiled warmly at her.

A little silence fell between them, punctuated presently by the car's horn.

'Perhaps I was wrong about you,' Hugh laughed. 'Perhaps you were wrong about yourself. Vine, too. Perhaps if we stay here long enough, Yolande will actually drag herself in to see what's what.'

'If I thought that—'

'Yes, if I thought that, too,' he agreed.

But he made no effort to try anything out, instead he put his fingers under Constance's elbow and propelled her to the door.

Yolande pouted when she saw him, announced that he had had time to remove Consie's appendix and put it back again. But she said it confidently, confident of her beauty, and Constance got into the car and waited patiently while the doctor talked to Yolande from Yolande's side.

At last they left him, and Constance set out along the track to the artesian pool.

It was, as Anthony had said, still unchanged, and they picnicked from its banks, the blue water now bluer still from the blue Salvation Jane reflected in its depths.

'How warm is it, Consie?' Yolande called from her cushions to Constance kneeling by the pool's side.

'Beautiful. That glorious temperature on stone walls when lizards simply have to drop off to sleep.'

'What a description! Lizards! But it's given me an idea.'

'Yes, Yolande?'

'That heat, that *natural* heat, I do believe it could do me good.'

Constance had been thinking that, too, but she had hesitated to say it.

'Look at all the spas everywhere,' went on Yolande.

'But mineral spas, Yolande. This is artesian, remember.'

'Which could be a better miracle, who knows?'

'Do you really think you need a miracle, darling?'

'Yes, Consie, I need a miracle. And what's more, I'm going to stage one. Constance, I'm going in!'

64

CHAPTER FIVE

YOLANDE had very ably stripped to bra and panties; she had been right when she had told Constance she was expert at that. Quickly Constance did the same, but though she did not waste a moment, Yolande, with the aid of her sticks, was out of the car and manipulating herself down the gentle slope to the water before Constance could come forward to help her. There was a little splash, then an ecstatic: 'Oh, it's perfect, simply dreamy, no wonder the lizards like it!'

'That was sun-soaked walls, silly,' giggled Constance, joining her. She felt pleased that Yolande had taken the initiative. This lovely hot artesian water could do her no harm, and, who knew, it might do a lot of good. She was not asking for miracles, as Yolande was, just a benefit or two would suffice, but if a miracle came along ...

She felt no apprehension. Though Yolande had been a hothouse flower and very opposed to sport of any kind, she still had been a strong swimmer, she recalled. She looked at the girl floating now in the steaming water, her pale hair spread out around her like a river hyacinth, the sun beating down on her exquisite face and finding not one flaw.

'You're lovely, Yolande,' she said impulsively.

'Not bad,' Yolande grinned back. 'And my legs, Consie, they're still the same.' She splashed up with one.

'Darling, to make those huge ripples you had to

move the leg quite considerably,' Constance said excitedly.

'I know. Yet I did it easily. I suppose it's just buoyancy, but I still did it as if I was normal again. Consie, do you think—'

'I'm no expert, but I'm sure this heat would loosen you up, relax you. All the same, we'll make haste slowly, dear. That will be enough for now. Keep floating while I go to the bank and find a suitable spot to roll you out again.' Constance already had found it, it had been the first thing she had done after she had plunged in, but she wanted to make sure that the bank surround was firm and safe, also to have Yolande's canes in readiness.

She swam over and everything was perfect.

'Time's up,' she called gaily, 'swim over to me.' Then she turned to a pool without any girl at all.

For an awful moment Constance knew nothing but blind horror, blind disbelief, blind panic. Then her vision cleared and she saw that there *was* something. It was a hand. In the few seconds since she had left her, Yolande must have turned on her back to do as Constance told her, but in the turning her foot must have caught something, or rather something caught her foot, and the log, or branch, or whatever it was, had tugged her down. Ordinarily there would not have been any log, any impediment at all, but there had been rain, weeks of rain, and vegetation had sprung up where vegetation had never been seen before. Even an insidious waterweed could have occurred in the pool, hot though it was.

Constance dived in. She was not a spectacular swimmer, but she considered she was a solid one. But she had no illusions as to what lay ahead. Though Yolande was pencil-slim, she was tall, and tiny towns, as Yolande had categorized Constance, need telling inches themselves to deal with height. She swam to where she had seen the hand and dived under.

The water was clear, but even down here very blue. For the first time Constance cursed the Salvation Jane and its bright glister. She could have done with colourless water, she thought.

However, she found Yolande immediately, and, thankful that the girl had been under only an instant, thankful that there could be no numbing effect with a temperature like this, she began to strain up.

It *was* a strain. Whatever had caught at Yolande was determined to prison her. It came frighteningly to Constance that the only way she would ever free the girl would be to free the weed first, but to do that she had to let Yolande go, and once she let her go—

Yolande still had been submerged for quite a safe period, but there was no time to waste. Constance made a last desperate bid to pull her, desperate since she shrank from releasing Yolande to dive further down, and at the same time she heard the knife-sharp parting of waters at her side. Something flashed by her, and foolishly she thought of stories she had read about monsters who lived in pools, who dragged you under. She held Yolande even tighter.

'Let her go, you damned idiot!' If it was a monster it spoke the same language as Constance did. 'I've freed her. Now I'll bring her up.'

Constance saw two entwined figures pass her,

thought stupidly that it all seemed like something in a water ballet, then seconds after felt hands now on her. She was towed to the bank and pushed unceremoniously up. She lay where she had been put for a moment, then she leaned on an elbow and looked round.

Yolande was there. So was the monster. Only the monster was Anthony Vine, though he could still have passed for a monster. He was supporting Yolande, but the eyes he turned on Constance flashed with rage.

'Yes, she's alive,' he said, answering her questioning look, 'and so, it seems, are you.'

Nothing else was said then. Yolande had closed her eyes. Constance had lost her tongue. Presently he got up and carried Yolande to his car that he had drawn up beside the Holden.

'Her clothes,' called Constance, finding words at last. 'Yolande's clothes!'

'You can bring them. At least you should be able to do that. And Miss Searle, I'll see you in the office as soon as you get back.'

She followed him in her car, but she did not attend the office at once. She wondered how he would have reacted to her two wet pieces of apparel, bra and panties, and nothing else. However, she did not shower, as she would dearly have liked to have done, since the waterweed . . . it had been waterweed . . . had left several stubborn green stains on her skin.

Instead she dressed in the first clothes she put her hands on, ran a comb through her wet hair, and that was all.

She went down to the office and knocked on the door.

'Come in, Miss Searle,' he called. He was sitting at his desk, and he looked up and nodded her to a chair.

She decided to get in before he could, but he waived any words of hers aside after her first few syllables.

'I've had it all from Yolande – how you're completely blameless, how you're the thoughtful angel – the rest. Her story, of course. I admit she might have surprised you by jumping into the water, but it was you who took her to the artesian pool, and made it all possible, so I can't pass that over.'

'No,' Constance said.

'When I didn't see you around the centre, when you didn't come to lunch, when I asked the kitchen and they reported that you'd taken a hamper, I didn't have to be Sherlock Holmes to guess where you'd gone. To the unchanged place. You don't like change.' He looked hard at her.

'No,' she said.

'So I followed and prevented a tragedy. However, as it happens, everything seems to have turned out fairly well, if no thanks to you. Yolande, anyway, is suffering no repercussions . . . *now*.'

'Now?' she queried.

'Now that she is the first patient ever in Corporation hospital.'

'Is she?'

'I thought, and Hugh thought, it was advisable to keep her in bed where she can be watched for a while, and there she lies, lapping it up as a kitten laps cream.'

Constance had her head down. I suppose that's how

you've been considering it all the time, she thought to herself, inability to walk has merely meant a grounded pet to you, something to be fed cream. She had to bite her tongue to stop her saying it aloud.

'Well, all's well that ends well,' continued Anthony Vine, 'though I can't exactly pass *everything* over, and I think you would be the first one to agree.' He looked sternly at her.

'Mr. Vine, I admit I did take Yolande to the pool, that it was entirely my idea, but I never thought ... I never dreamed ...'

'No. But next time think.'

'And dream?' Now why had she said that?

He looked at her quickly. 'Are you a dreamer?'

'I ... I don't know.'

'Then be sure before you make such rash statements. That, incidentally, comes from a dreamer.'

'You a dreamer?'

'Amuses you, doesn't it? Well, enough of this. Let's get down to facts. Tomorrow the female intake arrives.'

'Yes.'

'Among them, as well as the wives, as well as the clerical and domestic staff, as well as Sister and her nurses – Yolande's mother.' His voice was over-casual.

'Yolande's mother?'

'Yes.'

'Oh, dear, Yolande won't like that!' sighed Constance.

'Why?'

'She didn't want her mother. And surely' ... Constance felt a slow rage building in her ... 'what she wants at her stage of health should count.'

'Everyone wants their mother,' he said expressionlessly, 'I have no doubt you want yours.'

'Yes, I do.'

'Where is she?'

'In Fiji. My father deals in copra. But there are few occupations over there for girls, so mostly the daughters come over here.'

'I see. But you'd like to see her.'

'Yes.'

'Then why doesn't Yolande want to see her mother?'

'You should seek the advice of a psychiatrist regarding that, Mr. Vine. Perhaps you could even get one from the States,' she said sharply.

'When I do,' he came back coolly, 'I'll have two cases for him. A girl who should walk but can't. A girl who shouldn't talk but does. All right, you can go now.'

'Reprimand over?'

'Yes. You might call down and visit the patient, but I wouldn't advise a late session, we have a busy day tomorrow.'

'Yes, sir.'

'Sir now? Not even Mr. Vine?'

'Not unless you instruct me, sir.'

He let it pass. He even let her get as far as the door. Then he called: 'Miss Searle, was your mother pleased when you left?'

The question took her by surprise. 'I don't know.'

'I know,' was all he said. He waved her out.

71

Yolande was sitting up in the ward, and was certainly looking like that kitten that got the cream. She also looked quite breathtakingly lovely.

She greeted Constance gaily, and Constance secretly commended the Corporation boss and the doctor for putting her in hospital. There was no room for repercussions in the excitement that showed up like pink roses in Yolande's usually magnolia-pale skin.

'So you've come to visit the first patient ever in the Corporation clinic,' she laughed. 'Yes, that's true. There hasn't even been a casualty yet.'

'Are you feeling as good as you look, Yolande?' Constance asked.

'Like the girl in the song, I feel pretty,' Yolande replied.

'You always are.'

'But more noticeably in here lying on a sickbed. Seriously, though, Consie, I'm a fraud.'

'No underwater monsters dragging you under?'

'It was a weed brought on by the rains, silly. When you visit me next time bring another negligée.'

'Yes, Yolande, though I hardly think—' Constance had been about to say that she hardly thought Doctor Hugh, if the doctor was Yolande's goal, would have time to appreciate it. Tomorrow was arrival day, arrival, as well as of the wives, the clerical and domestic side, of the hospital Sister with her small staff. Hadn't Cressida been the Sister's name? Also – Yolande's mother was coming.

Constance did not know whether Anthony had told Yolande, but decided it would be better to mention it. Yolande taken by surprise could be very unkind if the surprise displeased her, and she had said she did not want her mother.

'Yolande—' she began.

'I know, Consie, dear Mamma is coming. Why, I don't know.'

'Yolande!'

'Oh, she's all right, I expect, but she's so like me . . . in nature, I mean . . . and I'll tell you something, Consie, if I wasn't me I'd loathe myself.'

'Oh, you fool!' Constance had to laugh.

She stayed with Yolande until Doctor Hugh came in, then excused herself and left. Yolande did not even see her go.

The doctor must have stayed with Yolande for the evening meal, for he did not come to the dining-room. That, too, had been Constance's intention, she had decided she would ring for a tray, get into her gown and have a quiet night. But when she rang the kitchen, she was told that she was expected in the restaurant, that Mr. Vine had selected a table and chosen a meal for two.

'Two?' she queried.

'You, Miss Searle, and himself.'

Constance put the phone down feeling very ordered around yet helpless to fight such authority, for after all he was the Corporation boss.

She did not dress up, though, hoping that would show him her distaste for his high-handedness. But even this was denied her. When she came down the stairs he was waiting in casual clothes.

'No penguin?' she asked lightly.

'No dancing lady?' He had looked her quickly up and down at once. 'We're both utilitarian tonight.'

'In practice for tomorrow.'

'Perhaps. I've ordered the meal. I didn't want Louis producing a long list of offerings for only two.'

'Yes,' agreed Constance, looking around the room, 'there are only two of us.'

'The engineering bosses and the geos, etcetera, are getting ready, too,' Anthony explained, 'getting ready to welcome their wives.'

'As we will.'

'Not quite the same.' He grinned at her. 'Our speech of glad-to-have-you will be at the airstrip, theirs will be pillow talk.'

'Pillow talk?' she echoed.

'Oh, come, Miss Searle,' he teased, and Constance flushed a vivid scarlet, comprehending too late and hating her naïveté, or so he must think.

The orchestra was not playing, so there was nothing to linger for once the meal was over. Anyway, as he had said, they were both strictly utilitarian tonight.

They finished with coffee, then he walked with her to the stairs. She wondered where a big boss slept in an undertaking like this and boldly decided to ask him.

'This will rock you,' he grinned. 'A house.'

'A house?'

'A functional house, in fact a rather sparse one just now. I always believe in leaving the homemaking bits to the little woman.'

'Oh, so you intend—'

'Yes, I intend,' he said, and he looked directly, challengingly at Constance.

She felt like retorting: 'Not that you'd notice,' but found that when it came to it she did not have the courage. Yolande might not be engaged as she had planned to be, but Constance felt she could scarcely say it to him without a lead-up to it first.

He climbed the stairs with her.

'No, I'm not a believer in hotel living, I'm essentially a family man.'

'With no family.'

'That can always be rectified.' Again that direct look.

They had come to the turn in the staircase; it was a beautiful flight, the tradesman must have been very satisfied with his work. Involuntarily, Constance stopped. And stopped Anthony with her.

'It was here—'

'Yes,' he said abruptly.

'She was running down the stairs and she tripped.'

'Yes.'

'Was there something wrong with the rug?'

'No.'

'Her slipper?'

'No.'

'Then—?'

'The story goes, Miss Searle, and I underline *story*, that she saw me coming and made haste too quickly.'

'To run to you?'

'Yes.'

'Well?' Constance asked defensively.

'Well, if that's to be believed, it must also be believed of Hugh,' he returned calmly.

'He was here?'

'We both came in together.'

'But it would be you she ran to, or tried to run to.'

'Why?'

'Because it was you she – she—' She did not finish.

'Well,' he said very levelly when he saw she wasn't saying any more, 'it isn't me now, and unless Hugh wants the happy?' . . . he made a blunt question of the word . . . 'ending that I did *not* want, he'd be advised to take the stand that I did.'

'You mean be hard, be ruthless, unsympathetic, cruel, think only of yourself?'

'Beware of pity, Miss Searle, particularly ill-founded pity,' he returned.

She stood looking down the beautiful stairs where a beautiful girl had fallen. *His* stairs.

She must have said so aloud, for he drawled: 'Yes, I never did deny that issue. Yolande has been well compensated.'

'Compensated?' she echoed.

'For something she hasn't lost, yes.'

'You mean, I think, the *specialist's* verdict that she hasn't lost. You mean her mobility?'

'I mean that.'

'But what about the compensation for the thing she did lose?'

'What do you mean, Miss Searle?'

'Compensation – for your love?'

He turned savagely on her, he was so furious that his leather brown skin had gone ashy grey.

'She never loved me. She just saw in me a man in a big job. A boss. And I, for what it's worth to you, never loved her.' He stopped abruptly, almost seekingly, obviously waiting for her answer.

'It's worth nothing to me,' Constance said distinctly back.

CHAPTER SIX

At nine the next morning the first female contingent put down on the Corporation strip. Everyone attached to C.C. had gone out to the flat paddock earmarked for the future Ukurrie Airport. It was far from complete yet, a terminal had to be erected and made attractive, but the essential factor of safety had been assiduously attended to, and the craft had no trouble landing on the runway, marked at this initial stage by white upturned plastic buckets.

The first plane-load was comprised entirely of wives. They climbed down into waiting arms, and from the length of time some of them embraced, Constance decided there would be no exchanges left for Anthony Vine's 'pillow talk'. How ridiculous that man had been!

There were fleets of cars and waggons waiting, and the wives were whisked off for a champagne welcome at the hotel.

'Champers at nine a.m.,' they laughed.

'Not every morning, this is a red letter morning for Corporation. The girls have joined the boys.' That was Anthony Vine. He could be very smooth for a cigarette-roller, for an outdoor man with leather brown skin and Salvation Jane blue eyes, when he tried. He instructed Constance to go in with the women while he waited for the next contingent, comprising the remainder of the wives and the clerical and domestic staff.

After that Hugh could take over, for the third load would be medical equipment and Sister and nurses.

'In that order?' Constance asked smartly.

'You're a sharp cooky this morning,' he commented.

'You are yourself, the women loved being girls.'

'Look after the girls,' he ordered, and strolled off.

Yolande, being hospitalized, was not in attendance. Constance doubted whether she would have been, anyway; Yolande did not like women en masse.

Constance jumped on the last jeep coming in, and by the time they reached the hotel had become friendly with several of the new citizens. But not a new young wife (she must be new, from the youth of her), for the child bride, scarcely any more, looked sulkily away every time Constance smiled across.

When they reached the hotel there were choruses of Ohs and Ahs.

'I told you so,' Mrs. Amberley, whom Constance recalled from her first stop at C.C., called triumphantly, 'I said that the Corporation hadn't forgotten anything.'

She was one of the more mature, dependable, experienced women, appreciated Constance, very glad to have her here; Rose Amberley was evidently used to uprooting herself to follow her husband, used to making the best of things, and that, even though C.C. offered the best, was what was needed now. For though there would be no hardship, no restriction, it was still a long way from home, from relatives, from daily papers, from supermarket specials, from things that women shrug carelessly over and pretend not to care about but still feel afraid to be without.

'It's going well,' Mrs. Amberley found time to whisper later to Constance during the welcome. 'We'll have a few misgiving souls here and there, that's only to be expected, but no drop-outs, apart, I should say, from Mrs. Grant. Yes, she's the young one, the sulky young one. Trouble there.'

Constance edged round the women, laughing more than usual because of the champagne to find the unlaughing Mrs. Grant.

'Let me fill your glass again.'

'It's not again,' the girl said.

'You didn't take any. That's a pity. It was to say "Happy to have you here." '

'Well, I'm not happy to have come.'

'No, but I guess we all feel like that at first, however, being reunited with your husband—'

'I could have done without any reunion.'

'You're a long way from home.' Constance started on another tack. 'It's all unfamiliar.'

'No, it's all too silly for words. Girls joining the boys.'

'But they are, dear.'

'Which,' said the girl quite rudely, 'is yours?'

Constance reddened. 'None. I'm not married.'

'Then you don't know what you're talking about, do you?' The girl turned her back deliberately on Constance, on all the gathering of women, and went into the garden. Mrs. Amberley, who must have been watching, caught Constance's eye and shrugged.

The second contingent arrived at the hotel steps and more champagne was poured.

Then one of the secretarial staff began allotting the bungalows. This was always a touchy procedure, knowledgeable Mrs. Amberley whispered to Constance, knowledgeable in previous undertakings; the wives of the younger executives always resented the wives of the seniors having a better home.

'All the homes are the same,' Constance reassured her.

'Which makes me wonder if the senior executives will resent the juniors,' laughed Mrs. Amberley. 'Not to worry, I do believe we're going to jell.'

The Sister and nurses did not come to the hotel. Hugh sent up a message that though they had been cordially invited they preferred to settle in first. Constance wondered how Yolande was taking the sudden presence of female hospital staff. She had a feeling that tonight Yolande would be back in her suite.

She was wrong. With the nursing contingent had come Yolande's mother, and Yolande, after greeting her, must have told her she could use her hotel rooms while she remained in hospital. Smiling a little at Yolande's predicament, a bevy of women or one woman, Constance sought out Mrs. Lawford to welcome her.

Her daughter might be like her in nature, but she was not in looks. Mrs. Lawford was an attractive enough middle-aged woman, but even in her young days would never have been in Yolande's class. Yolande was beautiful.

'You've been to see Yolande,' Constance smiled to Yolande's mother.

'Yes, Miss Searle. But just what is she doing in there?'

'In hospital?'

'Yes.'

Constance was a little nonplussed. 'Well, of course you know about her inability to walk . . .'

'Oh, yes' . . . impatiently . . . 'I know all about that. But she doesn't need a hospital bed to get her on her feet again.'

'I think we should discuss that later, Mrs. Lawford. Immediately you want to know why Yolande is in bed now?'

'Oh, I think I know really. To avoid me.'

'Nothing of the sort, Mrs. Lawford. Yolande had a bad shock, and I take most of the blame myself.' Constance told the story of the artesian pool as briefly as she could.

'So she has that to work on now.' The older woman firmed her lips. 'I'm sorry if I sound hard, Miss Searle, but that certainly is my eldest daughter.'

'You have other daughters?'

'Four others. And all' . . . proudly . . . 'married.'

'That's nice.'

'It's essential. A girl must be married. I've brought up my five in the expectancy of marriage, also in the striving after a successful marriage. It's galling to think that the best-looking of the lot has failed so far.'

Constance felt she had had enough for the moment, found something that needed her immediate attention, and turned away.

She went with the wives to their allotted bungalows. They all seemed quite pleased, but they would not have been female had they not cast estimating looks at the houses next door.

One wife did not cast a look, though, neither at the house next door nor her own house. Young Mrs. Grant said: 'So this is it,' then went and stood by the window.

'Most of the women have so much to talk about they don't want to come up to the dinner Mr. Vine is giving tonight,' Constance said, 'but the invitation still stands if you'd prefer to eat out.'

'No doubt Barry would. I can't cook.'

'Is Barry your husband?'

'That's what it says on the certificate.'

Constance gave a cheerful nod ... a determinedly cheerful one. 'So you can't cook? Now, that's wonderful. Yes, I mean it. There must be other younger ones like you, so we can be sure of a full attendance at our cooking classes. The hotel chef has very kindly agreed to donate some of his spare time. I'm confident even the good cooks will flock in, as Louis is a top-class chef.'

'Count me out,' Mrs. Grant said.

Though she had other women to settle in, Constance still lingered. 'You're the youngest of all, I would say,' she smiled hopefully.

'Shows my lack of sense.'

'Oh, I don't know, you don't have to be mature to know what you want in life. Look, dear, I know you're feeling strange now, but when your Barry comes ... it was Barry, wasn't it?'

'Yes.'

'Then everything will be different.' Where was Barry? Constance wondered. Why wasn't he around like the rest of the husbands? She knew that Anthony

Vine had allowed the men the time. She waited a moment, then asked: 'So you'll come up for dinner tonight?'

'I don't know. Do I have to say?'

'Why, no, but— Well, you'd want supplies from the store if you prefer to cook your own meal.'

'I told you I couldn't cook.'

'Also, we prefer to tell our chef how many. Surely that's reasonable enough.'

But there was no reaching this girl, neither with friendliness nor reason. With a little sigh, Constance turned away. Here was one character, she thought wryly, who could have done with a little of Yolande, not Constance.

Thinking about Yolande prompted her to make her way to the clinic.

In the short time since her arrival, the new Sister had made a hospital out of a collection of empty rooms. Constance did not see Sister Cressida Moore ... the sign on the Sister's office door already announced that ... but she had to admire the energy that had already put a different face on the place.

... And a different face on Yolande. Yolande looked anything but pleased with her lot.

'Hospital procedure, I loathe it. Hugh left me alone.' Yolande pouted.

'He was usually here when I came,' Constance pointed out.

'But it wasn't always hospital procedure,' Yolande said. 'That Sister is a pill herself as well as being a dispenser of them. She already has me signed up for a host of dreary, boring and probably very painful treatments. When she suggested physio, massage, exercise and what-have-you, I said yes quite happily, thinking there would be nobody to give them to me. But no, that paragon has all those arts herself.'

'Hugh said she was clever.'

Yolande looked sulkier than ever.

'It's all for your good, dear,' Constance urged.

'But I've had all those things. Anthony had every expert flown up to go to town on me, and what was achieved?'

'Those consultants were only visiting ones and could only give you a brief course. Sister Moore, being in attendance here, can spend weeks . . . months.'

'Perish the thought!'

'What's she like, Yolande?' asked Constance.

Yolande hunched her shoulders. 'Oh – aprony.'

'Like me?'

'Well, certainly not like me,' Yolande refused. 'Also she suggested a more utilitarian nightie for the treatments. Can you imagine me in flannelette?'

'It needn't be flannelette.'

'Well, neck to toe at least.'

'Oh, Yolande,' Constance laughed, 'it can't be that bad.'

'It's worse. You know my mother is here?'

'Yes, and I think it was very kind of Mr. Vine to fly her up; also kind of your mother to come.'

'And who,' Yolande asked plaintively, 'is being kind to me?'

A nurse came in with a bowl of soup and Yolande said: 'I don't want it. Take it away.'

When she had gone, Yolande complained: 'You've

been drinking champagne and I'm given barley broth!'

'You're in hospital, Yolande.'

'Yes, I suppose so.' A sigh. 'I suppose the only other alternative is up there with Mamma.'

'Yolande, you shouldn't speak like that,' retorted Constance.

'Well, I *am* speaking like that, and I'll tell you why.' Yolande pleated and unpleated the top of the sheet. 'In a way,' she said bitterly, 'it's because of my mother that I'm here now.'

'Here?'

'Here. Like this. Unable to walk.'

'Oh, Yolande!'

'It's true. It's years since I left home, admittedly, but in the years before, the formative years, my mother prepared the ground for all this. I don't expect you to understand, Consie, how could you from the comfortable background you had—'

'Wait a moment, Yolande, my family was barely comfortable. Certainly they were never rich.'

'You lived on a lovely island.'

'Yes, it was lovely, but the house was unspectacular.'

'Your father was an island trader.'

'A rather less-than-successful one.'

'Well, anyway, you didn't have an ambitious mother, made ambitious because she'd been left a widow and had five daughters to rear on nothing at all, a mother to drill into you right from kindergarten the importance of marrying well because poverty was so mean and rotten.'

'. . . But also marry for love,' inserted Constance.

Yolande laughed, and it was not a pleasant laugh. 'I can't ever remember love coming into it,' she said.

'Yet you've always liked men, Yolande, and not always successful men. I mean you did not demand to see their bankbooks first.'

'I expect every armour has a chink,' said Yolande, 'everyone has an unguarded moment.'

'I still can't understand you putting the blame on your mother.'

'I suppose it does sound far-fetched, but Consie, when you've been trained practically from the day you walked to look for material gain, it's hard to forget.'

'You mean—'

'Well, for instance, I mean I saw Anthony Vine but saw dollar signs all over him, not his rather nice face. Oh, yes, I saw that face too, I'm not entirely a lost soul, but his eligible state and the dollar signs stood out the most. Only' . . . that reversed horseshoe moue . . . 'it didn't work.'

'And what about – Hugh?'

This time Yolande did not have an answer. She sat back against her pillows frowning. Constance could see she was not sure.

'There,' she smiled, 'you're not such a loss as you think.'

'My mother wouldn't agree, she allows no chinks in armours, no unguarded moments.'

'Yolande, you're adult now, you've cut away from your mother.'

'Have I? *Have I?* Then why didn't I – why didn't I—'

'Yes, darling?'

'It doesn't matter,' Yolande said, and turned her head away.

Presently she told Constance she would like to go to sleep.

Constance went up to the hotel and was met in the lobby by Anthony Vine. It appeared that the chef had prepared a special introductory dinner and wanted all the new ladies and their husbands to attend.

'Most of them were looking forward to a meal for two,' doubted Constance.

'That can still be arranged, we have an abundance of secluded nooks complete with sweetheart chairs and romantic candles. I thought you could go down to the bungalows and persuade them. Louis was most upset when he learned that the party had ended with welcoming champagne. He informs me sorrowfully that he has a load of chantillys and dubarrys and what-have-yous more than half prepared.'

'Very well, I'll see what I can do, but I know one couple who won't be there.'

'Yes?'

'She's a Mrs. Grant. I don't know her christian name. He is—'

'Barry Grant.'

'You know him?'

'Of course. I know every one of my men.'

'There are over a hundred men.'

'So?' Anthony asked. When Constance did not comment, he said: 'I gather that Barry Grant was not there to greet his wife today?'

'No.'

'His own fault entirely, I'd given the men time off. However, he may be the shy type, prefer to reunite in private.'

'If he does that at dinner this evening he'll find his bungalow empty, for I think Mrs. Grant is coming up here – alone.'

Anthony Vine frowned. 'One thing I've left out of C.C.,' he admitted, 'is a marriage guidance counsellor. However, I still think you might be exaggerating. Probably Barry is all for skipping the meal and talking instead.'

'Pillow talk.' Now why had she said that?

She saw that he was laughing, not with his lips, but with mirth-narrowed Salvation Jane blue eyes.

'You catch on quickly, Miss Searle, do you think you'd catch on as quickly with the art of such talk yourself?'

'I couldn't say. Being unmarried, I've never been in that situation.'

'As far as I know you don't have to possess marriage lines,' he returned lightly.

He was teasing her, she knew, but somehow she could not banter back.

'That's an odd thing for someone to say, someone who told me that we may be in the middle of nowhere but it was still not the thing to sign up a lady in pyjamas,' she returned.

'Touché. I see I'll have to watch my tongue. If I hadn't been so censorious then I might have prevailed upon you now.'

'No.'

'Then – with a licence?'

'Licence?' she queried.

'Marriage lines, wedding ring, the rest.'

'With – you?'

'Yes.'

'No,' Constance said.

She turned and went down the corridor in as dignified a manner as she could, not helped by the soft sound of his teasing laugh.

CHAPTER SEVEN

Neither of the young Grants attended Louis's dinner party that night, but any supposition that they had dined together in their new home, talked together ... pillow talked? ... afterwards in the darkened bungalow was spiked by Barry's overseer's report that Barry had volunteered for overtime, then left later for the bachelor quarters.

Constance was there when Sam Carmody told the Corporation boss, and she saw the blue eyes darken with anger.

'Has he been applying for overtime all along, Sam?'

'No, Mr. Vine.'

'Then he can't suddenly start now. He can have his share, of course, but not when it pleases him to take it.' When Sam had gone, Anthony Vine turned to Constance. 'I don't like it. You have to expect disenchantment somewhere along the line, life's like that, unfortunately, but not right at the start like this.'

'I'll do what I can with Joan,' offered Constance sympathetically. 'Her name, incidentally, is Joan. I'll try to get her signed up for some classes to divert her. But' ... a sigh ... 'she won't be easy.'

'Perhaps when we have our first baby' ... Anthony Vine stopped and grinned. 'That could have been better expressed.'

'I know what you mean, though. You think Joan

and Barry will be influenced by a baby in our midst, then be encouraged to come together.'

'Come together? You really mean come together *again*, don't you? Anyway, it could be only a storm in a teacup and no drift at all.'

Constance shook her head at him. 'When I said come together I didn't mean come together again. Mr. Vine, I have a feeling, a pretty certain feeling, any coming together would be for the first time.'

'But they're married, Miss Searle.'

'Which doesn't necessarily mean—'

'My God, it does,' he came back with vigour, 'it damn well does in my book.'

'As a matter of interest,' she said coolly, 'what else is in your book?'

His eyes flicked at her. 'Would you like practical proof?'

'Verbal will do.'

'Then one man, one woman, one room.' He took out his makings and began rolling a cigarette, then lit it and put it in his mouth. 'One bed.' The cigarette was in his mouth as he said it, but the two words were very clear.

Again ... hatefully ... he laughed as Constance turned and walked off.

Apart from Joan, already the C.C. wives were 'jelling', as Rose Amberley had put it. Nearly all the classes were filled, and though midway drop-outs were to be expected, still this initial enthusiasm was a very satisfactory thing.

'A contented wife makes a contented husband,' Rose said. 'We have good conditions here, good pay, a good boss.'

'Yes, the conditions are excellent, and I've seen the salary scales.'

Constance did not mention the goodness of the boss.

Anthony Vine took all the wives out soon after their arrival so they could see for themselves where they now lived, why they lived there, what it was all about. Because the terrain fascinated her as no terrain ever had before, even the balmy perfection of the tropical islands of her young days, Constance went too.

The wilderness was still blooming, Constance found, and probably would for months, but eventually the ochre, the sienna, the burnt orange would creep back again, everything appear the barren waste that now was waste no longer, that gave back richer rewards than any lush pasture. Already the sparseness was making itself visible here and there by the occasional patch of gibber, by a drained salt pan shimmering like silver in the sun. Constance had noticed earlier that their town lagoon that had happened since her last visit was quickly diminishing.

The contingent of cars and jeeps let out its passengers, and Anthony Vine drew the women around him. He took out what looked like a schoolboy's magnet attached to a piece of elastic.

'The geos ... in fact everyone who comes bush ... carry this as you would carry a lipstick, ladies. If a rock around here proved magnetic, it could ... it also could not, mind you ... contain nickel.

'Mainly our C.C. geos look more formally for outcrops from subterranean rocks that through the years have come to the surface. That's their start. If tests are favourable then the whole C.C. business begins, technocrats come in, percussion drilling starts, and, with luck, we're in business.

'But that's only one of our more rare holes in the ground. Leaving the silica, we can come to bread and butter things ... well, you know that already from your husbands.'

They nodded, not over-anxious to hear a story they had heard already, for Rose Amberley had confided to Constance before they left that project husbands might not bring home briefs and estimates, but they still brought the equivalent, and that most of the women had come along today just for the jaunt.

One asked about uranium, though, and while Anthony Vine talked about control and stockpiling and being careful over markets, Constance looked around and saw to her surprise that Joan Grant had come, too.

She made her way round to the girl who was still standing by the jeep that she had evidently come in, and making no attempt to listen to what Anthony had to say.

'It's nice to have you join us, Joan.'

Joan shrugged.

'Interested in things like this?'

'No.'

'Well, secretly I don't think any of the ladies are, either. Now if it was a cave of precious jewels, or perhaps an opal—' She smiled.

Joan did not smile back. 'I'm not interested in either.'

'Yet you're wearing an opal ring, a very pretty one.'

For answer, Joan looked down at her ring, then without a word tugged it off and threw it along the ground. She climbed back into the jeep.

'Joan, your ring!'

Joan looked away.

Constance glanced desperately around for someone to help her search, yet to ask them would be to rouse curiosity, and she wanted no questions at this stage. She went in the direction she believed Joan had thrown the ring and began scouring a mental square foot by square foot. She wished the ring was something glittering to catch her eye; opals glowed but never glittered, except deep in their white or black hearts. In her absorption she did not hear the waggons and cars departing again until a voice asked:

'Are you working for Corporation, Miss Searle, or is this a strictly private digging effort?'

She straightened up and saw Anthony Vine standing quite close beside her. His was the only jeep left, and it was empty.

'If it's nickel you're after, I must warn you it's quite a costly process once you do find it. If it's uranium, we have a strict code here regarding it and you'd find yourself up against a lot of red tape. But if it's opal . . .' He opened his big palm and there lay Joan's ring.

'Oh!' The relief was so apparent in Constance's voice, he looked at her quizzically.

'That precious, is it?'

'Yes.'

'I haven't noticed it on you before.'

'No.'

'Meaning you've acquired it recently?'

'Yes.' She had no intention of telling him about Joan.

'I see. Then you'd better put it on. It's usually the safest way to carry a ring.' He handed it across, and unconsciously Constance put it on the accepted finger. She had not meant to, the movement had come instinctively, but at once his blue eyes became pinpoints in his leather brown face.

'We'll get back,' he said, and crossing to the waggon he climbed up to the driver's seat, then leaned across and opened her door.

They did not speak all the way back to the centre.

That afternoon Constance took the ring back to Joan.

'Oh, you found it,' the girl said without enthusiasm.

'Joan, it was a very foolish thing to do. It's a good ring. If you didn't want it, if it affronted you that much, you could have donated it somewhere. It doesn't serve any purpose throwing things away like that.'

'All right then, I hereby donate it to the deserted wives!' snapped Joan.

'There are no deserted wives at Corporation City.'

'By order,' mocked Joan, 'no deserted wives permitted.' She waited a moment. 'Then what do you call me?'

'You're not deserted. Barry may be living in the bachelor quarters, but Mrs. Jensen' ... Mrs. Jensen was in the next bungalow ... 'has told me that several times he has come and knocked on the door.'

'Oh, so besides being fed, entertained, ordered, lectured, hospitalized, we're now spied upon!'

'Joan dear!'

'Well, aren't we? Look, I don't want this ring. If you leave it here I'll throw it somewhere you can't find it.'

'I'll take it, then, until you come to your senses. It's an engagement ring, isn't it?'

'Well, it isn't a plain gold band and it isn't, and won't ever be, an eternity ring.' Joan gave a short hard laugh.

'But you chose it.'

'I had it shoved at me. For that matter I don't believe Barry chose it, either. He probably said: "One ring, and wrap it up, please." ' Again the hard laugh.

Constance stood baffled for a few moments, then she said: 'Well, dear, you'll know where it is.' She waited another moment, then left the girl.

She wore the ring for safety ... Anthony Vine had been right there, the most secure place was on a finger ... but the reason she chose the fourth finger, left hand, was simply because it was the only finger the ring fitted. She found that the corresponding finger on the right hand made it too snug a fit, and as for the rest of the fingers, they were either too slim or too plump.

As she might have guessed, Yolande's sharp eyes spotted the ring at once. However ... smiling ruefully ... she would have been even more obvious in gloves.

'What's that?' asked Yolande.

'An opal ring.'

'Oh, don't be facetious, Consie, I can see that, but who gave it to you?'

SEE WHAT YOU GET IN YOUR FREE MAGAZINE

Please answer the simple questions on the card, detach and mail today. We'll be happy to send you a copy of the 72-page Harlequin magazine absolutely free. It's our way of saying "Thank you" for helping us publish more of the kind of books you like to read.

Here's what you'll find in your complimentary copy...

● **a complete full-length novel**... lavishly illustrated in color.
● **a fascinating author's biography**... all the details on the exciting life of a famous Harlequin author.
● **exotic travel feature**... an adventurous visit to a far-away corner of the earth.

● **exciting recipes from around the world**... to bring delectable new ideas to your table.

● **special feature articles** on a wide array of unusual and entertaining subjects.